I0681658

Elizabeth York

Authors Note:

This story is more realistic than some you might read, but please remember it is fiction. There are a couple violent scenes and may not be appropriate for all readers.

Dedications

Dedicated to those I love the most, those who read the most, and those who have been supportive of me on my way.

A special dedication goes out to my betas, without you I think I would live in a paradise of self-doubt and depression. Thank you for showing me the way with each book on our journey.

Dear Daddy,

I thought of you today, but that is nothing new. I think about you every day and often make a wish that I could have just five more minutes with you, but it would never be enough.

I am grateful I got to share a little bit of my life with you, and know that you are in a better place. I know you are hitting home runs on the baseball fields in Heaven, and watching over your grandkids. You taught them well in your limited time with them and it has carried on.

They will grow to be kind, caring, respectful, and educated. All the things I am because of you. I hate that you are gone and the feeling I can't shake of always wanting you back, but there is no pain where you are, and that all I ever hoped for you.

I can't change the past, but I plan to change the future by living it to the max and making you proud of me every single day.

Love Always – Me.

 Support Cancer Awareness

Table of Contents

Prologue

"Hey Mom," I called out as I walked in the pale yellow living room with ugly blue shag carpet. "I'm here," I yelled out as I put my purse down on the arm of the brown couch and went looking for her. I heard voices coming from the kitchen so I walked around the corner and saw my mom sitting at the small four seater table with a man I didn't know.

"Kate," she smiled an uneasy grin as I walked in the room. She tried to get up, but she had been sick and it had taken its toll on her.

"Don't get up I'll come to you," I smiled at her. I walked over and placed a kiss upon her cheek and we linked pinkies – our own inside joke – then I turned to meet the man who was sitting at her table.

He looked nearly statuesque sitting there unmoving and staring uncomfortably at me.

"If you came to sell something, I don't need it. If you came to borrow something, I don't have it. If you came to date my mom, I guess if she likes you its okay, but I am the chaperone and she is home by ten," I rambled out trying to be funny, but the man with dark and gray hair and green eyes studied me intensly. "I was only joking," I spoke softly when his face didn't change. "I'm Kate," I replied and held out my hand.

As he took my hand in his to shake it, I noticed the gold Rolex which was gaudy, and expensive. He firmly gripped my hand as he shook it. It was all extremely intimidating, especially when he looked at me like he could devour my soul in the blink of an eye.

"I'm Henry," he finally said. "It is nice to meet you," he spoke with no emotion. His mono-toned reactions and tailored suit made me wonder what awful dating site she found this one at.

"Am I interrupting a coffee date or something?" I asked and didn't give anyone time to answer as I pulled my hand back and turned to my mom. "You told me to get off work at the garage early. You said we were going to dinner. I even went home and showered," I whispered.

"I'm in a dress, with no oil stains. Put that in your book of records cause it won't happen twice."

"I see that and you look lovely, Kate, and we are going to dinner, but we, well I want to talk to you first."

"Are you in some kind of financial trouble?" I asked as I grabbed a chair. "Do you need money, cause I can get another job."

If my mom was in trouble I wanted to fix it. Whatever was going on I wanted to be there for her, but my mom just kept shaking her head with every question. Then I looked back at the man again and then to my mom.

"What is going on?" I demanded to know as they seemed to pass messages to each other that I couldn't hear.

"Kate, this is Henry. Henry Huntington – your biological father," my mom spoke hoarsely and it was because of the rasp in her voice that I noticed the unshed tears in her brown eyes.

I turned and looked him over. There was no way I was related to this man unless there was some kind of generation gap thing going on. He didn't look like me, and he had barely spoken when I say ten words per second some days.

"Hi Henry, its nice to finally meet you," I spoke softly as my disbelief clouded my mind. He finally smiled at me and then spoke.

"It is nice to meet you too."

"Come on, we are all going to dinner," my mom called out and I stood up pushing in my chair and then went to get her coat.

"Should I call ahead somewhere?" I asked trying to think of anything to say so the uneasiness would fizzle out.

"No, my fiance already called ahead for a table at Le Bernardin," Henry stated matter of factly.

"The extremely high class and expensive French restaurant?" I asked and Henry nodded his head as we headed out the door. I walked my mom over to his car and the driver let her in. Then I turned to Henry. "Mr. Huntington," I started unsure of what to call him. "I can't afford to even drink their water. Can we go somewhere a little less extravagant?" I politely asked.

"Money will no longer be a concern now that I know about you. I won't let you be poor," he replied and I was a bit taken back by the answer, but I took a deep breath and remembered that when you take two people from two different worlds they have to learn each other before they can merge into harmony.

I was going to have to bend. We arrived at the restaurant I had passed a million times, but had never been inside myself. The décor was as extravagant as the people inside. Even in a clean charcoal dress I felt completely under-dressed.

"Mom," I whispered over her shoulder as Henry led the way. She turned her head and looked at me. "This is – I um – I don't know what to say," I spit out and she turned and stopped traffic to pull me into her arms and give me a hug.

"Give it a chance because it is better if you know both your parents rather than only one."

I wanted to tell her she was wrong, that I was happy with only knowing her, but I was somewhat curious about him. Henry had done nothing to tell me he was a bad person or that I wouldn't like him except for the way he looked at me that intense stare down scared the hell out of me.

Dinner was delicious, and the hours passed with ease as we finished the third bottle of wine. I was finally relaxed and everyone was getting along. I loved hearing Henry talk about his business, and art. He was so dramatic over the things he loved and I wondered if I had gotten that from him.

"You ever been fishing?" Henry asked and I smiled.

"Every chance I get," I responded and his eyes lit up.

"I love taking my boat out to the oceans edge where the thermohaline circulation is churning and the fish are jumping."

"Thermohaline circulation?" I asked. I had been to college, but I was almost sure if I tried to play that in some Scrabble or Boggle type game it would be wrong.

"The deep water current," he replied and his thrill seemed to fade. I guess now I looked like the dumb blond he probably thought I was.

"Do you like classic muscle cars?" I asked and the light in his eyes seemed to return. *Finally, a common ground subject I couldn't look stupid in.*

"I do. I actually own Classic Creations across the river," Henry spoke and I swallowed hard on the last bit of my food before the waiter took my plate.

"I work there with Mike," I splurged out with a little food still in my mouth. I quickly brought my napkin up and finished chewing.

"I know, your mom told me. It was quite a shock to know that my daughter was the one that I get rave reviews about."

My face hurt from the huge grin that had made its way there with the praise he passed my way.

"I love them, they just don't make the cars like that anymore," I replied and he nodded.

"I can buy you one if you would like," Henry offered and I choked on my wine. "Maybe make up for all the missed birthdays?"

Henry made me feel like I had known him my whole life. He seemed honorable and sincere, but when he made comments about him not being there when I was growing up I felt tense. In those moments, I was tongue-tied and couldn't find the right words.

This was like a fantasy. Meeting my dad was something I once wanted as a child, but grew to understand you didn't need a man around. However, him offering to buy me a car was like a sixteen year olds dream, but it couldn't be real. Things like this just didn't happen.

"No, you don't have to buy me a car. Really, it's not necessary," I stared down at the table while I answered. They brought out dessert and everyone else ordered a coffee while I asked for another glass of wine.

"Don't you think you have had enough?" Henry asked and I almost scoffed, but stopped myself. I would give him the benefit of the doubt since he didn't know me.

"This is only my fourth in the three hours we have sat here, I am not driving, and to be honest this is an unseasonable situation that alcohol can now say it helped bring harmony to."

There was no long a buffer between my brain and my mouth so I closed my lips, sealing them shut before I said anything I would regret.

"I'm sorry if I have made you uncomfortable, it was never my intent," Henry spoke like a gentleman. It was refreshing to see him back down like that because he didn't seem like the type to ever let anything go.

"I'm sorry. I am overwhelmed. I never thought I would ever meet you. I wasn't even sure if my mom knew who you were. We really never discussed it. How did you two even meet?"

I watched as Henry and my mom looked at each other. They seemed to smile at the same time.

"I met Henry a long time ago at a rock concert in the park. We dated for months, but eventually went our separate ways," my mom spoke softly as Henry put his hand over hers.

"Your mom was the most beautiful woman there and I just had to ask her out. It was a thrill when she said yes, but I wasn't the one for her. Her Prince Charming came while I was dating her. I wish we had stayed in touch, and I would have had a chance to see my daughter grow."

My mom looked sad, almost like it was a regret, but it was for the best. As they stared at each other having some memory lane flashback looking in each other's eyes I drank my water instead of the wine, and was content until I heard a woman speak behind me.

"You must be the whore who had my fiancé's baby," this blond over my shoulder stated and I jerked my head over to see her; ready to break her in half. "And you must be the slut who will take half of what's mine," she kept going as she turned toward me.

I pulled my napkin from my lap and slammed it down on the table. Then I felt a hand on my knee. I turned to look and my mom just shook her head asking me not to make a scene.

"Liza, that's enough," Henry spoke up and I looked at him in shock. This was the fiancé? The blond haired, enormously breasted, foul mouthed woman-child was marrying my dad?

"How old are you?" I asked and she smirked.

"Nineteen," she gloated. "What are you about thirty?" She asked trying to insult me.

"If I'm thirty, then what does that make your husband to be?"

Liza scoffed as the waiter brought her a chair and she sat down. Then the table got crowded as another man was given a chair beside her. What had started as Three's company was ending with Full House.

"Liza?" Henry turned to her. "What is the meaning of all of this?"

"I'm just protecting everything you worked so hard for," she baby talked him.

"What is all this?" I asked wondering what was going on.

"I'm Liza, your soon to be step-mom, and this is Adolf, our attorney. We gave you ample time to get to know one another and now we need to know what you want."

"I don't want anything except to know my dad," I gritted as I downed the wine. "Tell me Henry is this your doing?" I asked and he looked at Liza and in that moment I felt like the world tilted on its axis.

This man I had met had seemed like a wonderful person and I was eager to know him, but with a nod of his head and a single sentence I had lost all respect.

"I have to protect what's mine and Liza is mine," he growled. "I'm sorry Carol," Henry started and called me by the wrong name. I could feel my cheeks heating up as his words enraged me. "Liza is here to stay, and if you are like your mother you will be gone the second I give you a piece of jewelry."

My mom tossed a ring across the table and stood up on shaky legs.

"You all have to find a rhythm and work together because no one is going anywhere. No one is taking anything away from anyone, and just because it took me a long time to find the right man for me, that doesn't make me a whore."

My mom grabbed her jacket and I stood up with her knocking over the rest of my wine.

"I guess the apple didn't fall far from the tree," Liza said and it was the last thing she would say for a week as my fist contacted with her lip and it busted open.

"I'm sorry I met you."

Those were the last words Henry would say to me for a week and the ones that followed were not any better. Seemed as though when he chose Liza over me I became the child that was a thorn in his side, instead sitting beside his throne.

Chapter 1

"Hey Mike, what's in the shop today?" I asked as I walked in the garage. I often found myself visiting so I could sit in the classics, rev their engines, and feel the leather beneath my skin. I loved classic cars. They were my kryptonite, something I'd somehow inherited from the man whose condom had broken and made me.

"We got a '66 Fastback over there that just came in," he pointed over to a cherry red, Ford Mustang that was being prepped to be worked on.

I walked over to it, running my fingers across the hood as I closed my eyes and envisioned myself behind the wheel. I opened my eyes and grabbed the handle, opened the door, and climbed inside. I quickly shut the door, gripped the wheel, and envisioned the car was mine. I could almost feel the wind in my hair as I opened her up on the track. Could imagine her vibration from the horses revving to life.

This car was a wet dream for a girl like me.

"You're usually a Chevy girl. Are you coming over to my side? The Ford side?" Mike asked as he wiped oil and grease from his hands onto his coveralls.

I took in his beer belly, it had gotten bigger lately, and the silver in his hair shined brightly today.

I got out of the car, walked around the front of it, and lifted the hood. "I'm still a Chevy girl, but even girls like me walk the line when it comes to the 1966 Ford Mustang GT Fastback with the 289 V8 that produces 225 titillating horses. God, what I wouldn't give to own this car or even get bent over the hood for a classic tryst."

"I'm going to ignore every sexual innuendo you say about these cars. They are not toys that take AA batteries," Mike laughed. "This one isn't your dads, so no rendezvous, and I can't let you take it out for a joy ride."

I pouted my bottom lip and then laid back on the hood and stared up at the metal rafters.

"Couldn't you just see it? Taking it out to some deserted winery and parking to enjoy a picnic during the day. Then when the sun goes down, you lay on the hood and watch the stars make their entrance. Soaking it all in before you take her to the track and let her purr like every woman should late at night."

Mike merely shook his head and walked over to work on a blue Bel-Air. I climbed off the hood and wiped down the Mustang with a chemise, then ventured over to see what he was working on.

"Where did this one come from?"

"Guy who brought in the Fastback brought this one in too. His grandfather died and left him everything. He found these three cars in pristine condition in an old garage. It's a shame because whoever had them only took care of the interior and body. The motor has been sadly neglected," Mike replied.

I leaned over and looked inside the motor. "This is a 1955?" I asked and Mike began to laugh because the Bel-Air was my favorite car. I had wanted one for a long time, but I refused to ask my seed-dad for one. "This is a 1955 Chevrolet Bel-Air."

"You always talk about this one. You think you know it so well, can you figure out what is wrong with it?" Mike laid down the challenge and my entire body lit up.

"Ready for an education in classic cars from a girl?" I asked as I rolled up my sleeves and leaned in. I started looking for commonly known problems in the model.

"Oh, I'm ready. I think you just like to race older cars, but you don't respect their beauty. Besides, I've been looking it over for three days, you won't find the problem." Mike said.

Still looking at the motor, I replied, "This is a 1955 Chevy Bel-Air, in gloss black with white interior that looks like it rolled off the factory floor. That tells me this car wasn't driven much, which means any number of things could be wrong with it. Let's start with the engine shall we?" I took a deep breath and smiled as I saw what could be wrong. Mike watched as I started going through his unorganized boxes of parts and tools.

"Now I'm going to fix the car and educate you, so listen close. This car has a 265-cubic-inch overhead valve, V8 engine that was made to be smaller, lighter, and more powerful. It was also similar to that of the V8 in the Oldsmobile, though it carried a problem. In *this* model, you have what they called a 'y-block.'" I found an old part I needed, then walked it over to the car and grabbed my tools. I also grabbed a hair tie to keep my long blond hair out of my face, then leaned into the motor.

"You still haven't told me what is wrong with it. You merely described the engine. Guess the Chevy girl doesn't know everything about her dream cars," Mike taunted me.

I merely put my finger over my lips and told him to hush. "Mike, it saddens me to tell you this, but I know what is wrong," I stated sarcastically as I set to work on the car. "Bring me the hanging light please," I requested and Mike hooked it up so I could see better. The sun was going down and there was only so much light in a giant tin garage.

"What's wrong with it then?" Mike asked.

I pointed at the oil line.

"No, I already checked that."

"Tsk, you should listen to a woman who knows her cars. You see the y-block was tragically designed by your Ford company and severely flawed."

"It was not flawed," Mike stated indignantly.

He started to debate who had the better cars, so I grabbed him a metal chair to sit in and I began to school him once more.

"Bet me," I challenged. "You pay my half of the rent this month and I will fix the car."

"You are so on," Mike took my hand in his. "But if you can't get it running, you work with me on the cars down here every day for a month. I am back-logged."

He should have known everything about this model before bringing in a beautiful car like this, and especially before betting me. "I'll help you when my sperm-exploder isn't around," I agreed, and then we shook hands.

"Deal," we both said simultaneously.

I walked back over and began working on the car. I loved the feel of the metal and rubber sliding through my fingers. I was such a tomboy growing up, plus my mom went through so many men that I got a full education on classic cars from her boy toys, as well as from Mike.

"Mike, in *this* model with the block there is a deep yet tiny passage going from the crankcase to the cylinder heads. Finding it is as hard as a virgin finding a g-spot during his first time. It is possible though, if you know where to look in advance."

Mike burst out laughing at my comparison and shook his head as I ran my fingers along the tubing.

"You should remember that in 1955, oil was low on detergent and high on coke, so oil clogs were common and frequent. It was because of this that Chevy developed an external oil filter for the small block. It was released much later and most people went without it, as it cost them extra money to install. This car doesn't have one, and based on the condition it's in, I would say it was a Sunday driver. Short trips in this model are more likely to clog the passage than longer trips."

I continued working and allowed what I had said to sink in until I got sprayed with oil, successfully opening the clog. Mike and I both burst out laughing, then I walked over and hugged him with oil all over my red ribbed sweater.

"You are so passionate about these cars and you fix them with enthusiasm and eagerness. How are you not my daughter?" Mike asked.

I smiled at the praise. "I am no man's daughter. You see, my mom merely spit in a cup and out I grew. However, if I have to be made from someone, I would have loved it if it were you," I said with a sad smile. Then a cough sounded and I turned to see my sperm donor standing in the door.

"Hey Mr. Huntington," I stated as I went to get cleaned up.

"I have asked you a million times to call me dad, or Henry," My biological dad stated.

I turned back wondering how I wound up blond haired and blue eyed. He had dark brown hair with strips of grey and green eyes.

Maybe I was adopted and my mom forgot.

"Do you still have a wife not yet old enough to drink and get into clubs?" I asked disrespectfully.

"Liza has nothing to do with what you call me," Henry replied.

"Until you get a grown up wife, and have a family that doesn't border on statutory rape, I will call you whatever you want."

Henry took a deep breath and seemed to be counting to ten, but I was the queen of the whiny bitches so I counted too and when he got to nine, I spoke again.

"Why are you even down here? This is a work day."

"Your mom called," Henry spoke softly. "The doctor wants her to bring her family to her appointment on Friday. She has asked me to come."

His tone of voice made me wonder if they'd had an argument. "Yeah, I know," I quickly retorted, even though I didn't have a clue. "She has been sick for a while now, and they were going to do a scan last week."

"She was trying to find you because the snow has started falling and it is supposed to get bad. Do you need a ride into Manhattan?" Henry asked.

I nodded, then grabbed my jacket and walked over to Mike and placed a kiss on his cheek.

"I'm going to help you finish up those two cars. What time is good to come help tomorrow?" I asked Mike and he shrugged.

"Whenever you feel like it. If the weather does what they say, stay home. Don't risk your life for these cars," Mike smiled and handed me a bag of Skittles.

They were my favorite. You could eat them plain or put them in clear alcohol like vodka or rum and their flavor would be absorbed into the alcohol.

"These cars are my life. The snow won't keep me away. Only one thing can keep me from this place," I smirked and turned to Henry. "You are in your CEO tower tomorrow, right? So you won't be here, correct?" He nodded his head and I was sure he wanted to say something, but he simply bit his tongue.

I walked out and got into his brand new Porsche, that would never survive the snow, and silently rode the whole way back to the city. When we pulled up outside the apartment I shared with my friend Brooklyn, I went to get out when Henry cleared his throat.

"Wait Katie, I wanted to talk to you first," he called out.

I cringed. I was not a child, I was an adult and my name was Kate.

"What's up?" I asked as I breathed through my irritation. He turned off the car, got out, threw the keys to my doorman, and then walked me up the three floors to my apartment.

As we entered the grey-walled, modest floor plan two-bedroom apartment, I deposited my jacket on the hook and walked into my bedroom to put on another sweater. When I came back out, I knew something was wrong because he was looking everywhere but at me.

"Kathryn, I'm sorry to have to tell you this," he started.

I sat down and placed my hand to my chest, thinking it was about my mom.

"I'm going to have to let Mike go and close the garage."

"What?" I ignored the fact that he still couldn't get my name right and hoped he had an explanation as to why I'd just lost my job, and why Mike was losing his pension.

"Liza is pregnant and the garage is draining too much money during the winter. She wants me to let him go at the end of the season. Don't worry, he will get a severance package. I just wanted you to hear it from me."

"You are loaded. You own a penthouse and like, four houses or something." I yelled as I started pacing. "You said end of the season? Like two months away?" I asked and Henry nodded. "You know he can retire in seven months, right?"

"Liza and I decided that we didn't want to wait that long because the baby will be here by then, and it would be a lot to close it up after the baby arrives. Plus, you need to stop hanging around and working in a garage. You are my daughter and should act like a lady. So, starting Monday of next week, you will be transferred over to my building where you will be placed under my CFO. His assistant just got promoted so he needs someone."

I walked over to Henry, balled up my first, and sent a right hook directly into his cheekbone. He stumbled and immediately grabbed his face. Even with the sharp pain to my knuckles, I couldn't unclench my fist and wanted to hit him again.

"First, my name is fucking Kate. K-A-T-E! It's not Katie or Kathryn. Second, Mike will lose his retirement and have nothing for all those years. Seriously, I want to know who owns your balls, Henry?"

"Kate," he growled.

I wasn't having any of it. I clenched my already tight fist, ready to hit him again. "This is what you are going to do for being absent my whole damn life. You are going to get in your expensive, oversized, matchbox car and drive home. You are going to demand your nuts back from your wife and you are going to find a way to leave the garage open for both Mike and myself. Just because you knocked up some whiney, sniffling brat of a teenager doesn't mean everyone should suffer."

"Do not ever lay another finger on me. This is not up for negotiation, Kate, Liza is my wife. When you get married, you will understand that everything is a battle," Henry declared with a crooked sneer.

At that moment, Brooklyn used her key and came in the door. She took in his new bruise forming and my fist still clenched, and quickly moved out of the line of fire. She laid her stuff down and walked over towards me.

"This is why I will always be single. Who needs war in their relationships?" I screamed.

"You mean you will always be a whore," Henry called out.

I lunged for him, but he hurried to the door while Brooklyn wrapped herself around me to keep me from killing him. My rage fueled me as I dragged Brooklyn across the floor. By the time I got to the door with Brooklyn handing on, Henry had fled.

"Fuck," I shouted to Brooklyn as she let me go. I was still very riled up from my anger. "The man who gave me life thinks I am a whore and is about to take the things I love away from me. I wish my mom had never told him about me."

"Do you want to dance it out? We can order Chinese food and get wine. You know, make it a girl's night," Brooklyn offered.

Instead, I grabbed a pair of heels. "I'm going out." I shouted and slammed the door before Brooklyn could try to distract me some more. I didn't want her to comfort me or come with me. I needed a drink and a timeout from my life.

Chapter 2

"Do you have any idea what time it is?" Brooklyn shouted as she stood in the door way in her black tank top and pink pajama shorts with her long black hair up in a messy bun. Her cobalt eyes carried bags beneath them that said I must have woken her.

I tiptoed a little further into our darkened apartment. I thought if I could get past her I could get away without the lecture, especially since I brought home the man whose name escaped me.

"Tuesday? No wait it is after midnight so that makes it Wednesday, I think," I stated with a chuckle.

"Not the day, the time!" Brooklyn had that crinkle in her forehead that said she was pissed.

"March," I snorted and then couldn't hold back the incessant laughter that followed.

"Who the hell is this?" Brooklyn asked pointing to the man I had brought home.

"He's my next fuck up," I slurred my words, and then it seemed my brain wanted to function so I shouted to answer her first question. "4am. I think. Maybe."

I dropped the heels I was carrying to the floor and let go of the strange man's hand I was holding. "You look old when you're angry," I whispered at Brooklyn as I put my hand over my mouth to stifle my drunken antics then Brooklyn doubled in my vision and all the alcohol from my celebration was coming back up for one last hurrah.

"I was worried sick about you. Do you not know how to return a text?"

I bolted past her and bounced off the grey walls toward the bathroom we shared. I threw the door open and lunged for the toilet that was decorated in butterflies and books. There my body rejected every ounce of alcohol and hydration I had. When there was nothing left to be projected from me I laid on the bathroom floor and cried.

"Kate," Brooklyn called out from the doorway. "Drinking like this is not going to make anything easier," she whispered as she wet a washcloth, grabbed a towel, and laid it on the floor.

"I know," I gagged as I thought I was going to vomit again.

"I sent your date home," she seemed annoyed, but then she sat down and pulled me over to her where my head rested in her lap and my body rested on the towel. "You can't empty it into a bottle every time Henry does something to make you feel bad about yourself. Did you even think about talking to him rationally? Ever tell him how much it hurts?" She asked as she played with my hair and wiped the sweat from my body. I shook my head; almost afraid talking would make me puke again.

Brooklyn was my only real girl-friend. Lots of people want to be your friend when they find out your dad owns some million-dollar company that I didn't care to even learn about, but not her. She was like me; we both grew up with absent dads who sometimes did things we were not so proud of. We both had trust issues with everyone, but most of all she understood my weird sense of humor and awful drunken coping mechanisms. She just understood like no one else could.

"I love you," I slurred as Brooklyn sang me a soft song and toyed with my hair. I quickly drifted off to sleep surrounded by her comfort and warmth which was the opposite of what I had felt today.

"Good Morning," Brooklyn screamed into my ear. My head felt like it was going to explode.

"I think I am dying," I whispered with a sore throat, and a need to just sleep for a year.

"You can't die from a hangover, but I can make you wish you were dead," Brooklyn laughed and then began to beat a wooden spoon on a metal pan as the Ipod dock sounded out Five Finger Death Punch at maximum levels.

I covered my ears and begged for anything to make her stop. I normally would have wrestled the damn remote away from her, but I couldn't move without pain.

"Please," I begged, and cracked my eyes to see the smile on her face, and my mom behind her.

"You ever going to do this again?" Brooklyn asked as she turned the music down a little. My mom merely crossed her arms, and was going to let my brain splatter out of my skull and repaint the wall.

"No," I silently mouthed, and then without warning Brooklyn ripped my pillow from me to see my fingers were crossed beneath it.

"Right," Brooklyn stated. "You did that when we were five. Doesn't work now."

I nodded my head. *Yes, it did.* You never got too old for finger crosses, scouts' honors, and pinky swears. Life was too damn miserable to have to be a grown up all the time, so if I wanted to be a child she should let me.

"Brook," my mom called out, and they had some kind of hidden conversation. The kind where you knew she would bust your butt for something, but said nothing. She would only give you the eyes and then your ass automatically started to twinge.

"Yes ma'am," Brooklyn sweetly replied as she turned the music off. My mom took the pot from her and walked it out of my room. "You are so lucky she is here. Bring home another asshole whose name you don't know because *you refuse* to let me be there for you and I will make this hangover seem like a picnic in the park. Now get up and go hydrate."

That was my Brooklyn. When we finished college I realized how short life was going to be and tried to make it the most fun, while she went on to law school and became the bossy type. One day when she is like seventy and retires I will be the adult and she will be hitting up the bingo halls looking for a good time.

"It hurts," I whined as she opened my blinds to see the snow was falling and the sun was excessively bright.

"I'll bring you some medicine."

I sat up on the bed as my head throbbed to the same rhythm my heart had set out. I couldn't even hear over the pulsing in my ear.

Brooklyn had to tap my shoulder for me to open my eyes and take the pills.

"I have to go to work, but your mom is going to get you going and then Mike is expecting you," Brooklyn ordered before disappearing into the bathroom.

I got up and placed a hand on my head trying to shove the pressure back inside and keep my brain from becoming splatter paint. I smelled food and wanted to vomit as I rounded the door frame and walked into the living room.

"Kate," my mom called out. "Want to tell me why Henry called me and said you fractured his eye socket."

"I didn't hit him that hard. He is a liar," I protested, but the look on her face said she didn't care. "You know he is firing Mike before he can retire, and forcing me to be lady-like –*his words*- and work in his office."

My mom was so pale and skinny that I had a hard time seeing her like that. I tried to hide my fears that she was really sick, like antibiotics can't fix it sick, but I think she knew. I squinted under the throbbing pain in my head and sat at the bar on the wooden bar stool as I watched her scramble eggs. Then she scooped them out and added black pepper and ketchup.

"Do you remember when you started eating your eggs like this?" My mom asked and I shook my head.

"No, I just know you always made them like that."

"When you were little we went to a farm to get some hen eggs to learn how to make frittata. You got so upset when you learned where eggs came from. We gathered several different types of eggs, and made it a science lesson. That next morning you refused to eat the baby chickens that I had murdered –*your words*– and scrambled for you. Those eggs had cost an entire shifts pay, so when Mike heard he came over and brought you the pepper and ketchup. He let you add it to the eggs until you were convinced that it did not resemble a dead chick. Then you ate them up and have been finicky about them since.

"Henry didn't get to see that. He doesn't know that. I can't do anything about what he does with his business or his life, but I can tell you that carrying around anger is the same as eating plain eggs. You need to find a way to get over him being absent, and how you feel about Liza, and make it okay so you can move past this anger."

I didn't want my eggs, and just rolled them around on the plate. I was bitter that he was gone my whole life, but I didn't hate him until I met him. I saw a true chameleon in him, because after I met Liza I saw the colors change before my very eyes, and he would never go back. Besides I had the life I wanted; I had my mom, I had Mike for a dad, I had Brooklyn for a sister, and I didn't need the misogynist that donated his sperm to give me life.

"I'll try harder."

Those three little words had me riding shotgun on the first class flight into hell. I had lied to my mom, but she just seemed so frail I couldn't tell her I wanted him to die by a thousand paper cuts.

"Listen to me Kate," my mom started and then she placed her hand on mine. "I don't know what went on here last night, but I have never heard Brooklyn as worried as she was. She thinks you are spiraling and you are going to hit bottom. Then Henry called with the same concern and an injury. It is not like you to just hit someone without provocation. I taught you to fight back, not start the fight. Those two people care. I care. We all love you, so whatever is going on, let us help you."

I nodded and my mom laid a kiss on my forehead. I knew Brooklyn loved me, but Henry was the damn devil and didn't love anyone but himself and his twit. I even understood Brooklyn calling my mom, but for Henry to do it was more of him being a tattle tale and I despised narcs.

"I have to get to the garage mom," I smiled as the drugs started to kick in. I still felt like hell, but I would be safer there than here with Brooklyn's amp. "Do you want to come see Mike with me?" I asked and her whole face lit up.

"I'm not dressed," she started and I carefully took her hand led her to my room.

"Let's make you the beauty queen we know is hiding in there," I whispered and my mom grinned. She loved Mike and Mike loved her, but it would take an act from God to bring them together. They were both so afraid of losing the friendship they had made that they missed the fact that you are supposed to marry your best friend.

"Let's do it," she softly voiced her excitement. I knew she was trying to hide it, so we were going to make her gorgeous. Then she and Mike could take out the 55' and I could fix the Fastback.

For the next three days I worked on the cars while Mike spent time with my mom. There were moments when I wanted to ask why they weren't together, but love was fleeting. I supposed that was why they never went forward as a couple.

I was a conflicted person. I believed my mother was in love, but didn't believe it lasted for more than a moment in time. Whether it be five minutes or five years it always fades and someone always winds up crying themselves to sleep. Maybe I was damaged, or maybe I saw the big picture and didn't want the hassle.

Moments like now when my mom and Mike were laying on a blanket letting the snowfall on them. Like the world didn't exist outside the two of them. Like she didn't have a doctor's appointment coming up that could tell us of her fate. Watching them just be, made me believe I might be wrong about love, but then every morning after a night at the club when the guy tip toes out of my apartment or when I sneak out in the middle of the night to avoid seeing them again. Those moments made me believe in what was real.

"Hello," I answered the garage phone as its incessant ringing was driving me nuts.

"What the hell are you doing there? Where is Mike?" Henry shouted through the phone.

"Talk to me like that will make you hear a dial tone," I replied and I heard him take a forced deep breath. "Now, try again and act like your momma taught you manners."

"Kate," he growled and I waited until he was ready to complete his sentence. "You're fired. Get the hell out of my garage!"

Chapter 3

"It's too early in the morning for you to be up singing," I groaned. I could hear her on her way to the shower. I looked over at the clock to see it was early. *How did I get in bed?* "It's 5am," I shouted as I pulled the pillow over my head.

"Yea it is also Friday. If you don't want to wind up working under daddy dearest shouldn't you be looking for a new job? Your student loans will come calling soon if you don't."

"I have a job. It doesn't pay anything, but the rewards are phenomenal," I replied as I tried to snuggle under the blankets.

"What is your pretend job today?" Brooklyn asked and I sighed.

"I am a part time groomer."

"I am almost afraid to ask and I probably don't want to know. Who or what do you groom?"

I cracked one eye open and saw she wasn't leaving without an answer so I tossed the pillow at her. "I groom myself."

"I know what your problem is," Brooklyn spoke calmly. "Today is daddy day. You have to see him at your mom's appointment."

I shot her my middle finger and climbed back under the blankets.

"He is just my tadpole donor, and his name is Henry, not daddy." Since I hadn't had any coffee, my mouth exploded my next words like a volcanic eruption. "I mean, who even fucks a man named Henry? When you orgasm, do you fake them, count them, or is it like busting out in song, singing *'I'm Henry the eighth I Am'* by Herman's Hermits? It's all just so *gross!*"

"Yeah, sure you have no issues with daddy day," Brooklyn chuckled sarcastically. "I'm going to put on some coffee and I'll bring you a cup before I shower, if you want me to that is."

"No, I'll make it, now that I'm up before the sun," I stated, with a hint of bitchiness.

I went into the kitchen and started a pot of coffee, when I heard Brooklyn singing in the shower. She was singing 'Henry the VIII' and I felt like she needed something to cool her singing streak.

I filled up a bowl of ice water and walked into our little lilac bathroom. I then poured it over the white shower curtain that had butterflies all over it.

"You bitch!" Brooklyn screamed as her teeth chattered from the chill, and I smiled.

"Bet you won't sing it again," I laughed, but then she started singing louder. The song made me think of old people doing some kind of wheel chair sex or a horizontal polka. *ICK!*

Shortly after that, Brooklyn left for work and I was stuck pacing our apartment. The hardwood floors were ice cold since winter had decided to return in the form of a snowfall. I sipped my coffee as I stared at a wall, wondering what excuse I could use to get Henry to stay away from my mom's appointment.

The man never wanted me anymore than I wanted him to play the part. My mother and him had separated before she even found out she was pregnant and never told him about me, and after our initial meeting things had traveled downhill fast. There was no way I could work for someone like him. I'm a straight shooter and can't be around people that change based on who was around.

I took my shower and straightened my long blond hair, then put a few curls in the bottom, in hopes that he'd think I looked professional. I rummaged through Brooklyn's closet and found a black pencil skirt, a red silk blouse, and a black blazer. I was set to pretend I had found a new job.

I filled my black coffee mug that read, "If coffee is laced your safe. If coffee is not done you better run". As I walked out the door to catch a cab, Brooklyn called me.

"Kate," Brooklyn started talking, but had a bunch of voices in the background. Her voice sounded angry and muffled till she clearly said my name again. "Kate, the man with no name sent flowers to my office. Seems he thinks I am you and was waiting here for you this morning."

"Oh. My. God. Are you serious?"

"Oh yes, my boss is thrilled with an office full of I still want to fuck you flowers. Even better he must have been so drunk he didn't remember what you looked like because he didn't notice I have black hair and you have blond. Took me the last twenty minutes to convince him he didn't know me."

"I'm so sorry. I don't know what I was thinking going out drinking alone and bringing back strange men. I never break my rule to bring them home. It is always their place so they can't ever find me again. I am so sorry, honey. I don't remember why he thinks I am you."

"Kate, I don't need an apology. I know you needed to vent, I just wished you did it in a healthier manner, and left me out of it if I wasn't included."

"You want to be included?" I asked with a laugh trying to lighten the situation.

"I would only share myself for the right man, and you are missing a penis, so nope, no involvement for me."

"I had to ask," I smiled into the phone, but I knew the lecture was far from over.

"I want to keep you around until we are old and grey, but your choices are leading to an early death."

"I love you, Brooklyn. You are the only family I have that hasn't disappointed me, or been disgruntled because of me."

"I'm a little disgruntled now, Kate, but to be honest I think it needed to happen. I think you needed a wakeup call."

"You are the one for me," I joked trying once again to add a smile to her face, and lighten her tone.

"Kate, if we never marry by the time we are forty, do you think you'd want to be my wife?" Brooklyn joked.

"Only if my allowance has four digits monthly and you allow me a bi-weekly, one nighter with a real penis. That is the most I can stretch it. I need my bean flicked daily."

Brooklyn laughed and agreed as we joked through my cab ride. She always knew when I needed a friend and exactly what to say to put me back on the straight and narrow path I needed to be on.

We'd been wild together in our younger years, but law school and the loss of Mark, the man she secretly loved, had taken all her spontaneity away. I truly believed she lived vicariously through me, while at the same time tried to get me to grow up like her.

"I have to go. I'm here at Satan's door."

"Good luck my dear. I will be in court till noon, but if you need me, one of the bailiffs will get me. I will have Skittles, Snickers, and wine flavored ice cream ready for you when you get home. We can even sneak up to the roof and cook s'mores, since the last bit of snow has stalled. Whatever you want it's yours." Brooklyn replied.

I got out of the cab and tilted my head back to look upwards and see the building where Henry worked.

"You said the magic words, Brook. I'm going to take you and Henry, stick you in a mixer, then he gets a little of you in him."

"What do I get out of that?" She laughed.

"Another man's balls to hang on your wall," I replied just as a passerby fell into me, knocking my phone from my hand. The screen shattered on the sidewalk.

"Perfect!" I shouted. "Everyone is taking my lifelines. My job, my money, and now my phone."

"Sorry, but I need the cab," the man called out.

I ran and grabbed my phone off the sidewalk, then threw it at him. It bounced off the cab and landed on the street. I watched as the cab behind it ran it over, and I groaned loudly as nothing seemed to be going my way.

Someone should just shoot me and get it over with.

I was not far from the shopping district so I just started walking. I was going to replace my phone, deal with Henry, go work on the cars and take my mom to the doctor. This was the plan. I would etch my schedule in stone, but I think Murphy's law would find it funny that I made plans and roll my stone into the ocean to drown and never be seen again.

I wasn't far from the shopping district so I just started walking. I was going to replace my phone, deal with Henry, go work on the cars, and take my mom to the doctor. That was the plan anyway.

Four blocks later, I was standing in line at AT&T. Some new phone had come out and people had flocked to the store like it was the zombie apocalypse and they were the only place left with ammo.

"Hello, and welcome to AT&T. I am Darby, how can I help you?" The tiny little round woman asked me.

I nearly sighed out loud that she had manners. *Thank God someone in this city was still nice.*

"My phone got ran over." I told her and she led me to the computer. I was thankful she didn't ask many details and was quick to get everything shut off on that phone.

"I'm sorry Ms. Huntington, it seems we don't have any more iPhones in stock. If you want to wait we can order it for you and have it delivered in a few days, or you can transfer over to the Samsung Galaxy S7 edge," the sales woman spoke sweetly.

"I have to have an iPhone."

"I'm sorry Ms. Huntington, we just don't have any. The closest one in-store is in Albany," the sales lady replied.

My irritation grew. For a split second I felt like a toddler being denied a piece of candy.

"You don't understand, I need an iPhone, I know how they work. I've always been an Apple girl. That's the same as driving a Dodge and then going to a Chevy; it might have been acceptable in the 1990s, but since Ford bought them out, it's no longer something you do. That's like the difference between rich and poor, foreign and domestic, or even skirts and jeans. I need my iPhone!" I babbled on and on, unable to help myself.

The woman scoffed and walked over to talk to her supervisor. I watched as they conversed and knew I wasn't getting a new iPhone. When she returned, I listened to the same customer service speech I had given a thousand times when I worked in the mall when I was in high school.

Against my better judgement, I wound up getting a new Samsung, but they discounted it and showed me how to use it. I guess it really wasn't *completely* different, though I would really miss iTunes.

"That will be $245.54." The sales woman smiled.

I went to reach into my purse when I realized that it and my coffee mug were both still in the cab. I tried to explain my situation to her, but no credit card equals no new phone.

Brooklyn was in court and I didn't remember her assistant's number without my contacts. My mom couldn't afford it and it would take Mike an hour to close up shop to come help, especially when Henry was four blocks away. So I did the only thing I knew to do, I called my dad for help.

This was going to suck.

I used the stores phone and then waited on a bench inside the building. I watched the people go by for over an hour until Henry's driver finally pulled up. The driver simply walked inside and paid for my phone, then came over to me.

"Mr. Huntington expects your presence in order to thank him. Please come with me to the car," the driver spoke. I rolled my eyes but walked out the door and climbed in the car.

I arrived back at his office building and took a deep breath as I walked inside. I rode the elevator up to the seventy-second floor and walked out to see one of Henry's blond secretaries jump up to greet me. I had a bottle of water, a coffee, a neck rub, and brownies before I could even take a breath.

"Send her in," Henry's voice called out and I was thankful that his barracudas finally stepped away.

I swallowed hard and closed my eyes. With my new phone in my hand, his errand girl opened the door and I stepped inside. I looked over to his desk and saw my purse, coffee mug, and broken phone.

"How did you get those?" I asked with confusion.

"I had my security team go after it," he replied as he hurried into his jacket.

"That doesn't tell me how," I retorted, my attitude showing as I placed my hands on my hips.

"I had them review the footage to find the cab number, then they called the cab company to have the cab return. The man who knocked you out of the door no longer works here and you have your things back. The end."

I walked over and grabbed my things. I was about to say thank you when Henry started talking again.

"Kate, I had the ladies wash your coffee mug and refill it. You and I will need to have a discussion when we get back about your future here, but if we don't go right now, we will be late to pick up your mother."

Oh shit, how could I forget my mom?

The hours had apparently flown by from when I'd walked to and waited at the store. I had completely forgotten about my mom, content with feeling sorry for myself. I was chomping at the bit to be the worst daughter of the year.

Chapter 4

"Mom, are you nervous?" I asked. She shrugged her shoulders, then changed into a gown and attempted to climb up on the table. She was so thin that I could see the outline of her bones. Her skin was nearly translucent, and she could barely keep down anything. Everything seemed to hurt her; she winced as I helped her on the table. I pushed her graying brown hair off her shoulders and wrapped my arms around her. "Just us soda pop girls," I whispered, and hugged her to me.

"I'll be cherry and you be coke, cause no one needs a root beer float. As long as I have you and you have me, together we will be as sweet as iced tea. Sing out loud and give it a whirl, no one can defeat a soda pop girl," my mom said in a sing-song voice as we finished a creative hand jive and interlocked our pinky fingers, just like we used to do when I was a little girl with pigtails.

"You okay?" I asked as I turned to open the door and let Henry in.

"Kate, I'm sick," she said out loud and chills covered me. I turned and looked at her, my arms crossed to hide my chest quivering, and I had a sudden urge to cry at her words. Henry walked in silently and sat across from my mom, a look of worry on his face, which did not help ease my fears.

"We both have to face it. I have been sick a really long time, but no one was ever able to figure it out. When a doctor calls and says to bring in your family, that is the time to get your affairs in order."

I walked over to her and wrapped her in my arms again and told her I loved her over and over again. I couldn't help but feel like this was an omen of things to come. Her admission, and the darkened room. I could almost see death lingering over her and it scared the hell out of me. I just repeated I love you and held on so tight that I didn't even notice when the doctor entered the room.

"I would like to give her a quick exam, if you and Mr. Huntington would like to wait in my office," the doctor said.

I didn't want to let her go. I held on until Henry pulled me away and practically dragged me into the doctor's office.

"If she needs organs she can have all of mine. I mean, she did make them in her stomach's easy-bake oven," I spoke aloud because my brain to mouth function had no filter. I looked over at Henry, who had not looked up from his phone, except to move me, since we had come into the office. "Better yet, we can give her one of yours. That way you can contribute something other than the batter."

"Kate, I know you are nervous, but please sit down and stop pacing," Henry pleaded as a second phone dinged. I walked over and pried both phones from him and turned them off, then balled up my fists.

"Kate! I am still your father, learn some respect!"

"My mother should have spit," I grit out through my teeth. "If she had you wouldn't be here."

"Are you two getting along?" My mom asked as soon as the door swung open. She was dressed in baggy clothes that barely stayed on. Her frailty was so evident that when I leaned back up, Henry immediately stood, took her arm, lead her to a chair, and helped her sit down. It was the nicest thing I had ever seen him do.

"Am I too late?" Brooklyn questioned as she barreled into the room, completely out of breath and covered in sweat.

"What are you doing here?" I asked and she walked over and gave my mom a hug.

"I hope you don't mind me being here, Karen," Brooklyn whispered as she took my mom's hand in hers and looked over at me. "I'm family too. I want to be here to support whatever the doctor says. If you need blood, I got a little Russian in me. I will gladly send some your way. You know we make the best Vodka right? That has to count for something."

"I'm glad you're here Brook," my mom patted her hand.

We all took a seat and held hands, except for Henry. He was turning his phones back on and placing them in his pockets. The doctor walked in and sat at his desk. The silence was deafening and seemed to last hours. I was ready to explode when he finally started to talk.

"Karen finally came to me a few months ago. She had diligently been writing down every symptom with date, time, what she ate, weight, and the days' activities. This has been incredibly helpful in trying to determine what has been happening to her."

The doctor opened the chart and pushed a button on his intercom. The nurse came in a few moments later with a folder that seemed to be one-inch thick. The pale, white haired, heavy set doctor placed his glasses on his face and read over whatever was on top.

"It is what I thought. Karen, your levels have dropped again. With the weight loss we were finally able to see what the issue really is. Your scans showed four masses near your colon and in your intestines. We want to admit you, go in, remove them, and have them biopsied."

"Doctor," I spoke up as the room fell eerily silent. "What is happening to my mom?"

"Your mom has IBS, irritable bowel syndrome. It is really common condition and there are meds, but nothing really makes it go away. Since your mom developed it, she has dealt with the inflammation and side effects from it. That is why she didn't notice anything different until she started dropping massive amounts of weight. When these masses swell, nothing is able to get through. It is essentially forcing her to starve to death because her body won't accept more food."

I felt Brooklyn squeeze my hand and I tightened my grip on my mom's hand. With each word he spoke, I could feel her getting weaker.

"What is the prognosis?" Henry asked as a tear streamed down my mom's face.

"If they are merely benign cysts, we can remove them and start her on anti-inflammatories. We would then do vitamin therapy to get her healthy again, and we would routinely check to see if they return."

"That was the best case scenario, right?" I asked. I needed to say something because I didn't understand why he'd stopped talking. Everyone looked at me like I was insane, but I wasn't processing any of the information. It was hitting me like ammo hitting a bulletproof vest. "What is it you're not saying?"

The doctor walked around his desk and knelt down in front of me. He seemed to be just as emotional as I was. It was refreshing to find a doctor who cared, but his concern was showing and that scared the hell out of me.

"If it is malignant, with the location, size, and latest lab work, we may be looking at cancer."

"Talk to me as if she was a car. I understand cars," I pleaded as the dreaded 'C' word floated across the room.

"Kate," Henry began, "this is like the rust on the body of a car. If she has cancer, then think of it like when you bondo one part, only to find it had spread to five more places. If it is not cancer and just a group of cells, then it is like the clog in the gas line. Someone just needs to figure out if she has a clog or if she needs body work," Henry tried his best to explain, but repeatedly tripped over his words.

"Kate, what he means is, this could be a very simple fix, or it could be a fatal one," Brooklyn whispered as she took a tissue from her purse and passed it to me.

"My mom is going to die?" I asked the doctor as I looked at my mom. She'd already accepted her fate; I could see her slowly coming to terms with it. "When will she be admitted?" The doctor finally looked at me and merely put his hand over mine.

"I would like her to be admitted immediately, but Karen and I have talked about it and she would like to take some time to prepare. You can bring her in anytime tonight or tomorrow morning, but she has to be here by 6am for her pre-op. No eating after 8pm, and for today, try and stick to a liquid diet."

Fuck being strong, I couldn't breathe. We always know that the circle of life happens. My grandma died which left my mom next in line to get the ax, and then it would be my turn and so on. But she had struggled her whole life. These were supposed to be her years to relax and enjoy. These were her golden years.

Henry stood and helped my mom toward the door as the doctor asked for a moment with Brooklyn and I.

"I wanted a chance to talk to you both," he started as he went and sat back at his desk. "I want to level with you. You need to keep her in high spirits. If her levels keep dropping at the rate they are, she will be too weak for surgery. The sooner she walks in the doors to the hospital, the better it is for everyone. I know you have a lot of questions, but please ask them away from your mother. It will be hard, but only focus on positives around her for the next twenty-four hours."

"Just do your best. She means everything to us," Brooklyn demanded that he do his best, but what if his best wasn't good enough?

I got up, leaving Brooklyn and the doctor in the room, and ran. I kept jogging down the hall, looking everywhere for my mom. I finally saw her getting into the elevator with Henry, so I hit the fire exit. I flew down the stairs as sweat poured from me, I nearly fell in my heels but I had to get to her.

I barreled out the door when I hit the first floor and headed straight for the elevator, only to find that running in heels makes you slow because Henry was already putting her in his car.

"Wait!" I shouted, then ran out to her as I took off the blazer that was now sticking to my skin. The light snow fell around the overhang, and a chill hung in the air, but it didn't faze me as my heart struggled to catch up. "Mom, you have to go now," I started and she leaned over and put her fingers on my lips.

"I want you and Brooklyn to have a girl's night tonight. You are not spending the night in some hospital when you are young, single, and old enough to party. These are the days when you are supposed to go out and enjoy what you have. You don't want to wake up and think back on what you should have done. One day, you won't be any of those things. The time it takes to go from having it all to losing it all flies by in a blink of an eye. I am going to take care of some paperwork and pack. Henry will to take me when I am ready," Her voice was very weak and I started to protest.

Then she held up her pinky and I linked mine with hers as the tears flooded my face.

"We are the soda pop girls. We are strong and sweet. We are a sight to see and a tasty treat. No one can bring us down. We smile, never frown. We are soda pop girls."

I closed my eyes and she wiped my tears. She was going to do it her way and there was no talking her out of it. I hugged her to me gently, and then stood up as she held my hand and the cold weather finally hit me.

"Henry," I called out as he looked over the car at me. I don't think I had ever seen him care about much. So, I swallowed every ounce of pride I could and spoke to him as I always had, with threats.

"You have three hours or I torch your house. Get her admitted quickly so we both don't lose what we love most in life."

He flinched at my words, but I knew it wasn't over.

"Stop being overdramatic, act your age Kathryn," he shouted as he climbed in beside my mom and the driver shut his door. I wanted to correct him once more about my name, but instead I let go of my mom's hand, gave her a kiss on the cheek, and then closed her door.

I shivered as I felt my heart shatter cand waited till they were out of view to let my emotions out. I dropped to the ground as tears overwhelmed me and I didn't know how to stop them. There was not enough liquor in all the bars in New York City nor was there enough men to take this away.

"Kate," Brooklyn called out as her arms wrapped around me and pulled me off the snow covered sidewalk. "I know," those two little words from Brooklyn's lips to my ears were the smallest form of comfort, but it meant everything.

She lost her mom when she was little. I knew she had been through what I was dealing with, but even with her arms wrapped around me the cold had invaded my thoughts and I felt completely alone. Frozen in time, while the rest of the world passed by.

"I need some air," I whispered as I pulled her off of me. I put my blazer back on, and took my coat off her arm. I placed it over me and went to hail a cab. As a cab pulled up I turned and saw tears in Brooklyn's eyes and for a split second I felt bad leaving her. She was losing the only mom she had had since her mom died, and I couldn't comfort her. I was no use to anyone, so I would just go and do what I did best.

Chapter 5

"Kate, what are you doing here?" Mike asked as I slowly dragged my feet into the garage. "Did you have traffic court today?" He asked as he took in Brooklyn's suit I was still wearing. I didn't even bother to make eye contact as I walked straight for the car I loved.

"I'm gonna work. It is what I do best," I responded without emotion and concern shadowed Mike's face.

I opened the door and sat down in the Bel-Air. The white leather bench seat was as cold as ice, but it didn't bother me. I looked in the rearview mirror to see the beast that my tears had made. With the red eyes, pink nose and crimson lips from the crying I truly looked like a clown. I used my hands and wiped the mascara off my face and laid my head back as Mike climbed in the car.

We sat in silence for nearly twenty minutes as I leaned my head on his shoulder. I needed his support and he gave it to me when he didn't even know what was wrong.

"They said my mom is sick," I explained when I sat back up. He had known she had been ill, but saying the words out loud made it hit home with me once more, and Mike looked like he just lost his best friend. "She doesn't want me at the hospital till morning. She busted out the soda pop girls so I wouldn't fight her."

Mike smiled through the pain. I knew she was the only woman he ever loved, and now she was sick. If I couldn't be there for her tonight, then he should be.

"Sounds like your mom is still being her ornery self," Mike replied and an idea hit me.

"Go to the hospital, Mike," I started and he gave me a look that said he could cut through my bullshit. "You know you want to see her. She wants to see you. And if anything happens you have me on speed dial. I can take the Hummer and sleep in the parking lot." Mike looked like he was thinking about it when I whispered. "She needs us. Whether she wants to admit it or not she needs her family right now."

"Henry will be upset if I close early," Mike brought up a good point, lucky for him I was great at thinking in stilettos.

"I know the cars, and how to read the invoices. Just point me to what needs work done and I will close up at 8pm like you do. Then I will take the Hummer to the hospital and sleep in it. Henry cannot get mad because the work will be done. My mom will have someone there that's family, and I won't feel like an accidental pregnancy because I will be right outside even though she is pushing me away."

"Henry won't like this, Kate. I want to see my retirement," Mike said and I internally flinched. Obviously, Henry had not told him yet, and I didn't want to so I said the only two words I could think of.

"Fuck Henry!"

Mike gave me a crooked smile and I knew he was going. I finally felt like I had a reason to grin when I knew I had conquered this. I climbed out of the car and turned up the heater in the garage as I ditched the blazer. Brooklyn would probably be pissed that I was going to get her suit dirty, but I needed this.

We spent the next hour going over which cars were scheduled to be fixed tonight and which were being picked up. Then when we got confirmation my mom had checked in, Mike headed to the hospital.

The hours had slowly ticked by as I struggled to find the problems with the cars with my mom on my mind. I had called every hour until my mom unplugged the phone in her room. Mike had been one step ahead and taken the keys to the Hummer, because he didn't want me sleeping in a car all night.

I should go home and get some sleep, but sadly I don't think my worry-filled brain would allow me to relax enough to sleep.

Ten more hours and they would have my mom in surgery.

I struggled with an Oldsmobile, and finally just threw my wrench when I couldn't get a broken belt untangled. Frustration had taken a firm grip on me and wasn't letting go. All I wanted to do was pace. I felt like I should be doing something, anything, to help my mom. I hated this feeling that her fate was something out of my control. I hated not being able to fix this which made me want to go to the bar and drink it away or find a cock to ride so I could have a moment of bliss.

I was too deep in thought that I didn't hear the knock on the garage door. I had started to chew on my fingers when I heard a voice.

"Your fingers taste good?" A man asked and I froze like a deer in headlights.

"How did you get in here?" I asked as I immediately pulled my hands behind my back. I had just been thinking I needed a man, a quick fix. It would make the hours pass by and I wouldn't be dwelling on it, but who the hell was he or did I even need a name to fuck him? I started pacing again waiting for an answer.

I was just dropping off a car, but I saw the light on," this luxuriant man in a suit and tie started to explain and I halted my pacing and stared at him. The radio in the garage echoed through my ears as it started playing "Let's get it on," by Marvin Gaye, and I rolled my eyes at the coincidence of it all.

I will not fuck the hot guy. I will not fuck the hot guy. It will not make it better, so I will not fuck the hot guy.

"Do you know where Mike is? I need to leave him the keys."

I took in his brown hair that was parted like he gelled it for work, but had that messy look like he had ran his hands through that gorgeous hair all day. He was wearing a black suit with a red tie that commanded my attention. I felt like I was staring at the high school principal who wanted to know why I did whatever it was I did, only he was my age, and attractive, and I would not object to getting paddled over his desk.

"Ma'am," he called out again when I didn't answer. I shook the thoughts from my head and sighed as I looked down to see that I was covered in grease and oil. I was sure I looked scary, almost like if Deadpool and Wonder Woman had a baby and fed it to Elmo. The red and black shit that came out of Elmo would be the equivalent to what I looked like.

"Miss, are you okay?" The sumptuous man asked again.

"Sorry, was thinking about something. You can leave the keys with me I'm Mike's daughter," I lied and he seemed to relax from the situation. He walked over and held out the keys for me to take.

"Hello, Mike's daughter."

"Kate. You can call me Kate," I smiled as I took the keys from him. "What did you bring us?"

"1956 Austin-Healey 100/BN6," he replied and I had to force my mouth to close from the shock. I had researched, wished, and envisioned seeing one, but had never been up close and personal with it. It was my third most favorite car.

"The hundred was the first car from Britain to ever be able to actually hit a hundred miles per hour. There were only thirty-eight hundred and twenty-one of these cars that were ever made." I replied as the bombshell rolled through me that I was going to get to touch a car so rare they were auctioned off now.

"You know your cars," he replied with a crooked smile, and I wanted to swoon. I cleared my throat for no reason other than to bring attention to my throat. *Oh God, he looked at it too, bet he wonders if I swallow.* Stop it, I internally chastised myself.

"Where are you leaving her?" I asked and he pointed out front. I eagerly headed out to the front of the garage and saw a pale blue car being slid off the back off a tow truck.

"Wait!" I shouted as the wench sounded out. "Don't drop her here. Bring her around back and I will let you in. She can't be left out in the snow without shelter or a cover."

The tow truck driver started to whine, and I walked over to him and pointed my finger in his face and told him exactly how childish he was being. He still whined, but he did so quietly and I walked back inside to shiver from the chill I had caught.

"What's your name?" I asked as I turned on the brown haired man instantly when opening the back doors.

"Edward Wellington," he replied and a flicker of light showed me that his brown eyes had a sliver of green in them. That little discoloration was going to drive my OCD ass insane, but not in a I-have-to-fix-that way, but in a I've-never-had-that-I-want-to-fuck-him way.

"Well Eddie, I cannot believe you would bring such a beauty here and then leave her outside. What the hell is wrong with you?" I asked as the anger from the mistreatment of a classic finally set in.

"My name is Mr. Wellington, Edward, or Sir. Are you always this aggressive with your customers?" He asked and I curved my lips to the side in a scowl. He thought he was cute with that smirk on his face, but I was fucking adorable and he was about to figure it out.

"No, I am usually a delight until I meet stupid," I stated sarcastically.

"Maybe I should take my car to another garage," he chided out through gritted teeth and

I crossed my arms as I saw the tow truck backing up inside the tin garage.

"You could, but you will be back to have us fix their fuck up. You see Mike is the best at what he does and I learned everything from him. That means you have two people who will treat your car like a lady and get her ready to purr, but you have to be a gentleman with her and not leave her top less and in the cold like an ass-hat!"

"Now you listen to me little girl," he scolded and came to stand up against me. "I know how to treat a lady don't you ever doubt that, but this car is not a lady. You should know that an engine is female not a body."

"Is there an engine in the car?" I stammered with hostility as I stood on my tip toes trying to be eye to eye with him, but I was still too short. He had to be at least six foot something.

"Of course there is an engine in the car. I wouldn't bring her to a garage without one," he stated with sarcasm and a hint of attitude.

"Then she is a lady, and you are an ass-hat!"

"Mike knew we were bringing the car in late, and he is looking for a top as I didn't find one when I found the car," Eddie glared at me, and I decided it wasn't worth it to fight back. I walked over and picked up an invoice with a hint of bitterness. I threw it at him along with a pen.

"Fill that out, and let me know what she needs so I can fix her," I yelled as the tow truck driver closed the back bay doors. Then we were alone once more. I watched him closely as he started writing with his left hand and then switched to his right. Ambidextrous was a trait I hadn't seen in person before, and piqued my curiosity as to what else he could do with both hands.

The radio changed over to "Put it in your mouth" by Akineyle, and I turned and glared as if it could read my face. A moment later I was thinking about ripping his suit off on my way to my knees.

I couldn't take the radios taunting of the things I was denying myself. I had never once stopped myself from doing anything fun, not until I learned what I might lose. Funny how that works. I learn I might lose my mom and it makes me an adult and then I start taking stock of what is right and wrong, when my body just wanted to play. I quickly picked up a socket and threw it at the radio without a second thought in my head.

"What the fuck."

"I didn't like that song," I replied and he looked me over like he was sizing me up for a strait jacket. I walked over and picked up the pieces of the radio that were still singing about all the ways you could lick a woman and ripped the cord from the wall.

I walked over and placed the radio in a box near the office where I could see Eddie, but he couldn't see me. I fantasized about him pinning me to the hood of the car and then he interrupted the fantasy by talking. *It was not what his mouth was doing in my head.*

"Do you always stare at your clients?" He asked as he looked up at me and smirked. Little did he know what was going through my head where I thought he couldn't see me. I looked down and could already see the rosy blemishes that showed when I got aroused.

I had an itch the other night and somewhere between the tequila and Brooklyn it never got scratched and then this man walks into my garage when I need something the most. It just aggravated me more because it would never be enough, and it seemed I had grown morals in the last six hours.

"No," I replied hastily with anger and walked over to the red Mustang and wiped her hood down with a chemise.

"Are you always this angry or do you just presumably hate me?"

I looked back at him as he loosened his tie and waited for an answer. I stopped touching the car that drove me to fantasies that I should not be envisioning and walked over and took his invoice.

"I don't hate anyone," I replied with a sigh trying really hard to let it go, to let all my stress out with the exhale of a breath. "I apologize if I came off angry. I have a lot on my plate and have no time for handsome assholes who don't respect cars."

"You apologized and then insulted me. I think you should say you're sorry one more time,"

Eddie replied and I walked up on him and wrapped his red tie lightly in one hand then I pulled the tie till he bent down and my lips were near his ear. I let a soft breeze of warm breath leave my lips to his ear and then said the magic words.

"You are sorry."

Eddie pulled back and glared at me. I was almost having fun. I looked around Eddie to the Henley and saw that the buttons for the top looked almost new. They were glistening under the lights.

"You obviously need a spanking, but that would be crossing all those invisible lines we can't cross," Eddie spoke up with a growl and I stepped away from him.

"You'd have to catch me first, but any time you think you are man enough I invite you to chase me," I flirted as I walked over and opened the tiny hatch between the seats and pulled out a leather top that had never been used. I waived it in the air at Eddie.

"Found her top," I gloated as Eddie twisted his lips trying not to say anything. He was gorgeous. Stern, uptight, and ornery, but handsome and splendiferous. I looked up to see he had been with me almost an hour. *Holy hell time flew around him.*

"You should go, after all it would be inappropriate if I let you spank me," I smiled and gave him a wink as I turned away from him.

"Could we discuss your spanking over dinner?" He asked and I shook my head.

"You have to go, I need to lock up, and I don't trust ass-hats to be locked inside with me," I said with a serious tone. I was taking the conversation back to business only. "You can call Mike in a few days and see where we are, but you are not a priority for me to fix so it could take months," I explained as I walked away. He looked like he had won something which raised my guard as I watched him pull out his phone and call someone.

"Hey Mike, I am leaving my car with your angry and obstinate daughter," I heard him say and internally winced. I should have known if he was delivering late then he would have Mike's number. "No, delivering the car was easy, but being called an ass-hat was a little out of the ordinary," he continued and soon he held the phone out to me.

"Tattle tale," I mouthed as I took the phone. "Hey Mike," I spoke into the receiver.

"Kate, do you want to tell me why you are cussing at my most important client?" Mike asked and I knew he was going to be angry so I told him the truth.

"He was going to leave the 100/6 out in the snow with no top, and then -," I was cut off and walked over to the office door so Eddie wouldn't hear.

"Kate, I love you, but you can't be yourself around him. You have to bite your tongue. That 66 Fastback you love so much. The beautiful 55 Bel Air, those belong to him. Now be nice, make him happy, and get out of the garage. You should have gone home hours ago."

"How is my mom?" I asked changing the subject as I fiend for an update.

"She is trying to sleep, but the nurses are coming in and taking her vitals every hour. They had to come in and do her labs again. The doctor said at this time her labs are borderline with surgery being an option. If they decrease over the next couple of hours she won't be allowed to have surgery."

"What does that mean?" I asked as tears filled my eyes, and I felt my world slipping away. "What can they do if they don't do surgery?"

I started to tremble as I tried to hold back the sobs that were begging to be released. I didn't even remember Eddie was in the garage until I felt his hands on my shoulders. I turned to face him as a tear strolled down my face. I stared into his brown eyes as Mike's words stabbed me.

"Kate, honey, if they can't do surgery then they will send her home and allow hospice to come in and make her comfortable. I'm sorry sweetie."

I hung up the phone and handed it back to Eddie as the tears fell and I sobbed into my hands. He pulled me into his chest and I cried on him as he tried to soothe me. I felt safe and warm with him here, but leaning on a stranger was not something I did.

The sound of the tow truck honking as he pulled away broke the embrace. I wiped my tears and stuttered over trying find a plausible lie, but the words wouldn't come. Eddie wiped my tear off my cheek and whispered. "Sorry I ratted you out."

"I'm sorry," I stated as I pulled back from him and wiped the tears that had fallen on his tie. "I don't know you and here I am crying all over you."

"Sometimes the best place to find strength is in the arms of a stranger."

"Are you trying to get laid?" I asked with sarcastic laugh trying to cover up the new painful blow I had felt from Mike's call.

"No, just wanting to help. Scouts honor," he whispered as he held up three fingers. I loved that he could show a hint of childishness and allow me to hide what was beneath my surface. Made me feel like maybe he wasn't a major asshat, but he was still in the minor league.

"I can drive you home since your ride left, but if you try anything I will cut your balls off and hang them from my rearview mirror."

"Message received. I will make sure to keep my hand and feet inside the ride at all times,"

Eddie replied and for a split second it made me laugh. A few moments ago I was crying in his arms and now he was doing everything he could to make me smile. Maybe he wasn't an asshat after all, but we would find out on the car ride.

"Just give me a few minutes. Where do you live?"

"Upper West side, Manhattan," He answered and I nodded. Then I went about getting everything I needed. "You know I'm told I'm a good listener if you need to talk," Eddie stated as I grabbed my heels off the floor and climbed into the Hummer with him.

"Once I get her started I will turn on the alarm and lock up then I can get you over the river," I explained as I avoided his 'you can talk to me bullshit.' I had been through enough of that to know he wanted to get in my skirt. I leaned over and pulled the wires down to show the electrical tape from where I had hot-wired it as a teenager.

Truth was I wanted him, but I didn't want to use him. Weirdest feeling in the world. I had been this way my whole life, but a few tears on a tie and suddenly I wanted to get a house plant with him.

Then like a wrecking ball hitting a building a new form of pain slammed into me. I realized my mom had always wanted to see me get married and have kids even if I didn't believe in any of it, and now she may never see it.

I was out fucking around when I should have been finding my future family so my mom could have met them and then she could have been proud of me. Just the thought made me want to sob.

"You steal a lot of cars?" Eddie asked and I laughed through the new fog of depression that was hanging over me. Even through his humor I felt like I had lost a part of myself from all the things that were coming to light. Like what about when I became a mom and needed her. What about when I hit menopause, or if I ever got the big "C." What about all the times I was going to need her and she may not be there.

"I was a handful in my younger years. I did and said things I shouldn't have and there are reminders of it everywhere."

"I want it notated for the record that you are committing this criminal act alone and I am the innocent bystander," Eddie stated with his hands up.

"Do you ever loosen your tie, Eddie?" I asked with genuine interest and he frowned. Business suits were all the same uptight, over-worked, under-paid people whose brains were focused on work twenty-three hours of the day and Eddies one hour off was already up.

"Are you ever happy?" Eddie asked and my brows furrowed. Of course I had been happy, but that was back when dating was something you did with a chaperone, and illnesses were a myth. When there was nothing to fear because your mom guarded you with her life. Once upon a time I had been happy, it had just been a while since then.

"I'm happy," I lied and he read right through it.

"I'll loosen up when you stop being so angry."

I let it go, turning my focus back to what I was doing. I sparked the wires till the engine revved and Eddie climbed in the passenger seat and made a call to the tow truck company.

Unleashing some of that alpha male testosterone I knew lingered beneath his lapel.

I made some adjustments to the seat and steering wheel then I climbed out and turned out all the lights and the heater. I set the alarm on a delayed exit and then climbed back inside the Hummer. I pressed the garage door opener and the bay doors swung open to let me out. Then I drove Eddie home in uneasy silence because for the first time in my life I didn't know what to say.

Chapter 6

"Where are you headed?" Eddie asked as we headed into Manhattan.

"I'm going to drop you off and go home," I whispered not really knowing what to say to him.

"Want some company?" Eddie asked and it made me do a double take. I was in limbo between shock because he asked and curiosity wondering why he asked.

"I have a ninja for a roommate, pepper spray in my purse, and I have been trained to detach balls blindfolded on my knees with my hands tied behind my back," I went full Days of our Lives with my answer including hand gestures and faked fearlessness.

"I would expect no less from someone like you, but I was asking because I feel bad about making you cry. I feel like I owe you something."

"I wasn't crying because of you. I can promise you I don't shed tears over boys," I responded with all the attitude I could muster into those two sentences.

"Now I am a boy?" Eddie scoffed. "It is late, and you are upset. Find a place and we will stop."

"You are hell bent on getting me to go out with you aren't you?" I retorted sharply.

"Don't take this for more than what it is. I merely feel bad that you were in tears over something I may or may not have done, and I figure I better make it right because you are fixing my babies," Eddie spoke honestly and I thought it was kind of sweet so I lowered the barricade I put up so men can't get to know the real me.

He was attractive and I had done much worse, but I kind of felt like I was about to cross a line by allowing him to see me for what I was.

The only real problem was that if we stopped and had a drink would it lead to sex, and if we had sex, and I enjoyed those blissful moments where life happened in the background and I had no problems what would my mental state be in the morning? Then if morning came and I snuck out, and I headed to the hospital would I even remember his name? Or was I so far gone that even one night with Mr. Tie me up or Tie me down wouldn't hide my problems and they would come back with a vengeance when I came up to the surface to breathe again.

"No sex," I spoke up as if he had offered it when he hadn't.

"You don't know me so that comment is forgivable. You could march in my bedroom in a whip cream bikini and I still wouldn't give you my cock. I am not that easy. I say when and I say where that happens," Eddie's sarcasm couldn't be missed, and neither could the way his bedroom eyes looked at me when I finally agreed to go get some food with him. It was enough to let butterflies into my stomach, as I fought everything that came natural to me. He was as adorable as he was irritating, and arguing with him was already the most fun I had had in a while.

The hours passed as we sat at a twenty-four-hour coffee shop talking about everything except what mattered, and what was important.

I had discovered how he liked his coffee and that Clumsy Smurf was his favorite. I knew he was educated and demanded the attention of anyone who came by.

He learned that I have no filter and say what I think no matter the consequences, and that my favorite my little pony is Derpy.

As much as I wanted to say I was focused on my mom and everything happening around me, I couldn't. Eddie was a perfect distraction without the guilt and painful hangover. I think he may have to become my new friend for when Brooklyn is busy.

"Who is your favorite chipmunk?" I asked as I took another drink.

"Alvin," Eddie replied with a smile. "What about you?"

"Theodore," I replied and Eddie looked at me strangely. I knew I had just sparked a whole new conversation.

"Why Theodore?" Eddie asked with that my chipmunk is better than yours twinge.

"He is the one they underestimate the most. At the end of the day he is the one no one expects to be a bad ass, but he can save the day."

"I think you and I are watching two different chipmunk cartoons."

"I love the fact that you watch cartoons," I shined as I had finally met an alpha-man-child. I wanted to capture him and put him in a jar to keep him forever even if his taste in chipmunks was all wrong.

"Do you want another coffee?" Eddie asked and I knew I was close to my limit before my body started shaking with a caffeine/sugar overload.

"No, I think maybe I should get you home and then I need to go home. I have to be somewhere in the morning."

"It is morning," Eddie replied and I looked out the window to see the sun was cresting over the Hudson River. My stomach sank and I looked at my watch. I started counting the minutes I had left to the house and get Brooklyn.

"This was just what I needed," I whispered and Eddie seemed to know it because he just nodded. His attention was caught on something over my shoulder.

"Kate," a familiar deep voice echoed behind me. I turned and looked up at the brown hair blue eyed hockey player that I had once taken home with me. *Oh God, this was not happening.* I had to rack my brain to even remember his name. Kevin. Keith. Kyle. It was something like that then I thought of it.

"Hi Kurt," I spoke softly and kept my head down. I shouldn't feel uncomfortable, but I did. "What are you doing out so late?"

"We went out to celebrate another win for the team. Anytime you want to come watch us I will get you a seat." Kurt stated nonchalantly. "How have you been?"

"I'm okay," I answered in a uncomfortable whisper. "How are you?"

"I miss you."

"You don't even know me," I was nearly silent as I tried to hide my embarrassment, but I was sure my crimson cheeks were giving it away. I was never apologetic for how I lived my life, but I felt guilty and ashamed in this moment. I had enjoyed my time out with Eddie because there was no tension, stress, or strings attached. There were no expectations, and now he was going to think I was the slut Henry thought I was.

"I know your favorite drink is tequila rose. I know you only go to dark alcohol or beer when you are already drunk. I know how you taste. I know the sounds you make when you are turned on. I know that you need a man in control so you can just let go. I know your pussy tries to pull my cock even deeper inside you when you get close to orgasm. I know how you sneak out in the middle of the night with nothing of you left behind. I may not know your favorite color, but I know you."

Holy hell this was uncomfortable. Open up Webster and under the outlined word awkward you would see a picture of this moment for references. I couldn't stop the ill-at-ease feeling that flooded my veins when I realized Kurt wasn't walking away.

I ran my hand through my hair and looked over at Eddie who seemed to be sizing Kurt up.

"Kurt, that hurt," I cried out as he shoved me into the window making room for himself beside me. I turned and saw the murderous face Eddie was sporting and tried to defuse the situation.

"Kurt, I think maybe you have had a little too much to drink tonight and should cab it home," I whispered as I held up a hand to Eddie to tell him I had it under control, but from the look on his face he could read right through me and knew I didn't. In that moment I saw his transparency and knew I only had about thirty seconds before he turned into the alpha in this situation.

"Only if you are coming home with me," Kurt replied as he drank the rest of my coffee and wrapped his arm around my neck, dragging me to him, and placing a kiss on the top of my head.

I was never a damsel in distress, but I felt like it right now. When I dealt with men I was usually as drunk as they were and game for whatever.

"I think you should stand up, walk away, and when you sober up you can call the lady and apologize for acting like an ass," Eddie spoke up and I swallowed hard. He was authoritative and demanded attention when he lowered his voice like that.

Gone was the gorgeous gentleman and once again returned the sexy school principal who was about to give us all detention.

"I think you and I should step outside," Kurt stated as his words started to slur. His entire body reeked of alcohol and his actions said he was three sheets to the wind and probably wouldn't even remember this, but Eddie and I would.

"Let's go outside then," Eddie stated as he stood up, walked over, and grabbed Kurt by his jacket lifting him from his seat.

They shuffled around and I scooted a few inches up next to the window trying to put as much distance between me and them. I tried so hard not to watch whatever was happening, but my eyes were glued to Eddie. "Apologize to Kate, who you will never call again," Eddie stated as he held Kurt in a fixed position with his arm behind his back.

The look on Eddie's face was intimidating, I just knew he would snap Kurt's arm and not even blink. It was as scary as it was intoxicating. No one had ever stood up for me before, usually they are all harping on me, and I was standing up for myself.

"I'm sorry Kate. I'm really drunk and you can't just give a guy the keys to the castle and then tell them to sleep outside. I miss you and wanted my stronghold back."

"Now say goodbye," Eddie growled tightening his hold, flexing his biceps. Kurt didn't get to say anything as Eddie led him to the door. He opened the door and practically dragged him to the curb before letting him go.

They exchanged words I couldn't hear. It was a testosterone war, but I didn't know if it was about me, over me, or because of me.

I watched until Kurt leaned over and puked. Eddie hailed him a cab and forced him inside. Then he turned and came back inside the diner threw money on the table and held out his hand for me.

"Want to tell me what the hell I have gotten myself into having coffee with you?" Eddie asked and I shook my head.

The silence was irritating. I swear I could hear the words whore circling in the air just waiting for my ears to open up and absorb them.

"I don't owe you an explanation," I stated and Eddie merely looked over at me. "I don't apologize for how I live my life or how I cope with my problems," Eddie continued to look at me which made me feel like I had to keep talking.

"I went to a hockey game with my best friend Brooklyn and her friend Mark right after graduation a few years ago and I met Kurt. His team was headed to playoffs or whatever and they were going to trade him, so I took him home and thought that for one minute in time I could escape my life, and I wouldn't have to deal with the consequences because he would be gone. Only he didn't leave, he signed on for three more years since then."

Eddie continued to look at me. I didn't know what he wanted me to say. I had already said more than I wanted and more than I should, but his demeanor told me that he wanted an explanation and wanted it now. I wasn't capable of giving it to him.

"Thank you for stepping in. I don't know how that would have gone if you hadn't of been there."

"You're welcome," Eddie growled. Then he turned to look out the window as we headed toward his house.

"I'm not a whore!" I stated defensively, and Eddie's head whipped back around to look at me with confusion.

"I never said you were a whore," he self-justified. "I have never called anyone anything even remotely close to that. In fact, I wouldn't label you."

Guilt suddenly took control of my body. I was stressed that my mom was having surgery very soon. The one guy who I had known for only a few hours, but had assumed he could be a treasured asset now knew exactly what I did when I didn't want him to. I was putting degrading words in his mouth when he hadn't said anything. I had to end the night on a good note or Mike would hear every sordid detail.

"Want Skittles?" I asked as I pulled a bag from my purse. "I only eat the red ones, but you can have the rest."

"I want the red ones," Eddie grinned and all tension seemed to dissipate with his dimples showing. I hadn't noticed them before because I was hooked on his chiseled body I knew had to be hiding under that suit and his bedroom eyes that always gave me a come-hither look. *I bet he had a ten-year-old wife like my sperm donor.*

"I will give you half of the red ones," I smiled and went to open the bag while trying to hold the steering wheel. The bag popped and exploded everywhere. "Well that worked out just like I thought," I muttered aloud when I looked down to see Skittles in my cleavage.

Eddie burst out laughing and we rode the rest of the way to his place as if the night never happened. Everything I did around him was wrong, but he somehow made it seem like everything was going to be all right.

Chapter 7

"Did you get any sleep?" Brooklyn asked as I gathered my laptop, and other items into a bag.

"No, I tried, but the last twenty-four hours have thrown my entire life into a blender and every so often someone presses the button and I am just trying to breathe through it. You wouldn't believe what happened last night even if I told you."

"Does it have to do with this?" Brooklyn asked with a huge smile on her face as she pressed play on her voicemail.

Hi Brooklyn, my name is Edward Wellington. I am the ass-hat that Kate will undoubtedly tell you about. She told me about you so I am hoping you can relay a message to her. Tell her I hope her day goes better than the night did and that we switched phones. If one of you could call her phone later, set up a meet, then we can exchange them. Thanks. Oh and remind her that last night proved I know how to treat a lady with or without a top on, and she still owes me that apology.

"Not talking about it," I stated with a big grin spreading across my face. Brooklyn looked at me inquisitively but said nothing else about it.

"Get dressed, I will make coffee. I transferred everything yesterday to the partners so I could leave early and they will take care of everything today so I can be at the hospital with you. I called for a car to pick us up at 5am."

"Thanks Brook," I whispered as I walked into the lilac bathroom to shower. I knew Brooklyn was bogged down at work. They buried her under all the grunt work and silly hearings because she was never one to back down from anything. She never told them no. That made her taking time off a really big deal and I went from smiling at Eddie's voicemail to wanting to cry with the compassion coming from Brooklyn. I wasn't going to break. I would be strong for my mom.

I showered and put on a pair of skinny jeans with my knee high black Uggs. I paired it with a hot pink tank top and a black cropped sweater with a hood. Then I walked out to see Brooklyn wearing jeans and a black sweater, making me feel overdressed while holding my purse while on the phone.

"Can we do it on Monday?" She asked and I waited and listened. "Yes, I know where your office is. I look forward to meeting with you." Then Brooklyn hung up, but said nothing about it.

"What was that about?" I asked and she smiled.

"What happened last night?" She countered my question with a question.

"Are you wearing my favorite Uggs?" I asked and Brooklyn smiled.

"Did you wear my silk shirt to the garage and get it covered in oil?" She asked and I stopped talking because I knew I was busted.

"Want to tell me what the call was about since you already have possession of my shoes?" I asked with a hint or irritation.

"Ready to tell me about last night? You know I might give them back after today if you tell me," Brooklyn teased, but she was lying. I knew the tone; my shoes were gone. Like a bad breakup gone.

Both of us had questions while the other had answers. Seemed we would be at a stalemate, but curiosity kills the pussy and I had one that was dying to know.

"Eddie, Edward, whats-his-face that was dropping off a car for Mike and I to fix saved me from my drunk and horny past," I spoke softly not giving much away. Brooklyn tilted her head and I knew she wanted to harp on me about my drunken choices, but thankfully she didn't.

"You remember Taylor Cross? The district attorney. He called to ask about a meeting."

Taylor Cross was everything his name said it was. He was a man you didn't cross. His family came from money and influence. Years ago he was all over every paper as the youngest elected District Attorney in New York County. He never failed at anything if what the newspapers said was true.

I had only been arrested once and going up against him was scary. He was in the running to become the next District Attorney and was making examples out of everyone, but Brooklyn came to my side and helped me even though she was just a law student. I thought the way he looked at her was sexual, but maybe it was about her style of law. My charges were dropped so I never thought about it again until now.

"I remember him. I thought you worked in corporate law, is one of your clients in trouble?"

"No, nothing like that. He just wants me to meet with him. He said he needed fresh eyes to look at something and my name came up when he asked around."

"I don't believe him for one second. When you see him please remind him that I had you first."

"Really?" Brooklyn asked.

"Really! You and I both know a meeting with him means a date, and let's face it your legs have been welded shut since Mark started dating Mary. So that means it has to be a job offer and more time at work as if the twenty hours a day you do now are not enough. I had you first and I will have you last so that means there is no room for him or his job offer."

"Your maturity is missing this morning. Did you leave it in the shower?" Brooklyn asked with a smile.

"I left it in my other Uggs," I replied as I looked down at my shoes on her feet. I took the coffee cup she made for me and downed it in one gulp, like a triple shot. Then I poured another. It was going to be a long day.

"You ready to go?" Brooklyn asked and I shook my head.

"I want to curl my hair and apply make-up. Not sure if it is a good idea, but I want to hide the worry on my face if that makes any sense."

"I get it. You want your mom to see you as she always has and not as the worried little girl you feel like. I've been there, but it's just a little frosting. Your mom can see right through it."

"You don't think awful people who sin a lot can burst into flames entering a church do you?"

"Kate, you are not a bad person, you just have bad judgment, and I have never heard of anyone bursting into flames or anything else walking into church."

"Then can we swing by the church? I need to light a candle this morning, and say a prayer for my mom," I asked and Brooklyn nodded her head.

I sat at the vanity in our bathroom and got ready as memories flooded me of my mom getting ready at a similar vanity.

An hour later, I was sitting beside my mom as the nurses scurried to get everything done to take her into surgery. Henry had not even bothered to show which was probably for the best.

With my mouth and his lack of respect there was sure to be a fueled amount of hatred which would not be healthy for my mom.

"Mom," I whispered as I picked up the hand that didn't have an IV in it. She looked up at me and tried to smile, but her exhaustion was evident. Her body was so emaciated that she could barely sit up to see me.

"I know you are worried Kate, but I will be fine. We are stronger than most women because we are the soda pop girls. So, no matter what happens today you will always be the cherry to my coke."

A tear strolled down my face and dropped onto her hand. We both looked at it and then she held out her arms and I curled up beside her as I had done a million times before when she was too tired to walk to the bedroom after her second shift of the day.

"Ma'am you are going to have to get up so we can take her upstairs," the nurse said as soon as my mom wrapped her arms around me. I reached up and showed the nurse my middle finger. My mom laughed as the nurse scoffed and left the room to go tell on me. *I was engulfed in a world of adult tattle tales.*

"Kate, she is just going to come back in here with more people." My mom stated with a saddened tone.

"Let them, I have a finger for them too."

"Come on sweetheart, if it is time then it is time," my mom whispered and I took the message as if she was no longer talking about surgery. I climbed off the bed and turned on a dime to stick out my pinky finger and she locked hers with mine.

"You are the whipped cream and cherries to all my sundaes," I whispered as I laid a kiss on her forehead. "Promise me, that when you feel tired, or want to give up that you will think of me and borrow my strength to get through it. I'm not ready to let you go. Selfish as it is I am not ready to be an orphan."

My mom brushed my blond hair away from my face and said those words that made me want to punch a wall.

"You will never be an orphan as long as Henry is around."

I wanted to tell her he was an asshole. I wanted to tell her that I hated him and everything he stood for. I wanted to point out that he didn't even show up when she needed her family the most, but instead I shook my pinky with hers and laid a kiss on her cheek as a stampede of orderlies came to remove me from her side.

"Mike is family too Kate, don't forget that," my mom whispered, but I would never forget. I loved Mike and as I caught his view in my peripherals I could see he loved us too.

"I will be right here when you wake up," I shouted as they scurried around my mom and got her out of the room. I followed until they took her up in the elevator. I stared at those silver doors for what felt like an eternity.

"Kate," Mike called my name from behind me and within seconds I felt his hands on my shoulders. "Let's not wait here as if it is goodbye. We can go to the waiting room and wait to say hello again when she wakes up."

"I love you Mike," I whispered as I turned and wrapped my arms around him.

"I love you too baby girl," he replied and held me there while I struggled to get my emotions under control.

"Why didn't you ever marry my mom?" I asked and Mike released me to step back.

"Because your mother deserved better than some mechanic. She has always been worth more than I could ever give her."

I merely shook my head as we headed to the waiting area. Some men just didn't understand. We don't care what they have to offer us as long as they love us and treat us with respect. I guess those are some lessons that are never learned.

The hours were unhurried as my impatience wore on. I swore the clock was laughing at me at one point when nothing changed in what seemed like an eternity then it jumped ahead nine seconds all at once.

Brooklyn sat in the chair going over files she had brought and typed up briefs while we waited. She was a workaholic. She was never one to back down from anything and it worried me, but she always seemed to come out on top.

It is the very thing that made her a great attorney.

Mike was asleep with a coffee in hand as his head leaned over on the top of the seat. Even in dreamland his worries laid across his face. I hoped he was dreaming of fast cars and faster women, but as his brow creased I knew that wasn't the case.

I looked down at my half empty coffee cup that was half filled with cold coffee. I was bouncing my leg with a need to know what was happening and yet I was eternally grateful for them not to say anything. No news was always good news in our house.

I thought back to the first time my mom brought a man home. I couldn't remember his name, but I remembered his smell. They had dated for six months before she brought him home to meet me.

She guarded me and kicked him out when I knocked over a drink and he flipped the coffee table. I climbed into the cabinet to see what would happen with my stuffed rabbit. He only hit my mom once, and then she grabbed the cast iron skillet from the stove and swung around and hit him.

Mike came and the police were there. Then I remember seeing my mom with a bruise on her face as she sat down outside the door crack.

"Kate, baby, I wish you would come out and just let me hold you," she whispered, but I was terrified. "That man can leave bruises on my face, but he can't hurt me because I have you and you are all that matters to me," she shed a tear and I cracked the door open to see Mike come and sit beside her.

"I won't ever let another man hurt you or your mom," Mike promised. Then I climbed out and my mom pulled me into her lap. She sobbed on me and Mike held her tight. I remember we had a long talk about snakes in tall grass and how not all men were like that, but I remember as she tucked me in that night the last thing she said to me and I still held it close to me.

"My life only matters because of you."

I snapped out of memory lane and wondered where Henry was just long enough that he showed up. It was like Beetlejuice, I thought about him one too many times and he showed up.

"What is she doing here?" I asked as I took in the blond on his arm. Her breasts were so big I was shocked she could stand up straight. I wonder if I bumped into her in her red summer dress if she would fall and pop them. I should do it because mother nature has a tight hold on the cold, even today it is snowing, and yet she is wearing anything that shows off her boob job.

"She is your stepmom," Henry spoke up as if that was supposed to mean something to me. The only thing she was a mother to was Henry.

"Careful Henry, they don't allow children under twelve in the waiting area. You may have to take your wife to the nursery first."

"Is that how we are going to play this game?" Liza asked as she walked over and stood in front of me with her hands on her hips.

"I don't play games, those are strictly for kids," I replied as I rolled my eyes. I turned my head over to Henry and asked again. "What the fuck is she doing here?"

"I wanted to come and be supportive," Liza replied as she rubbed the tiny bump on her belly. No way was she six months pregnant. She was merely bloated from her period. "You know you could be nice to me I am carrying your little sister in me."

I nearly gagged. I didn't want to know what alien she had inside her and I sure as shit didn't want it sharing my DNA. Poor kid would grow up so deformed, deprived, and desperate that even the make a wish people couldn't fix that.

"Brooklyn is my sister and she takes up all my time. I have no room for another."

Liza scoffed and walked over to whine to Henry about how rude and unhinged I am. It was a weekly argument and I might have listened if she had a driver's license or could buy her own beer.

Mike woke up and came over and sat down beside me. I leaned my head over on his shoulder as he sipped his cold coffee. He understood when I needed someone with no words spoken. Kind of reminded me of Eddie a little.

Liza walked over to Brooklyn and cleared her throat. Brooklyn moved her stuff so Liza could sit down beside her. As if there were not a hundred empty chairs around us. I swear this woman was annoying to us all just for shits and giggles.

"I'm going downstairs to swap phones with Edward," Brooklyn spoke up as she read a text.

I could almost feel him in the building. Like my body was attracted to his. Magnets, that was the only way to describe it, but he wasn't on my list of things to do today.

Thirty minutes later, Eddie walked in with Brooklyn and spoke to everyone. I noticed he showed up in jeans and a New York Yankees t-shirt. Seeing him outside the suit and tie was a little odd, but it was a nice change. He walked over to Mike and shook his hand. They spoke about cars and dirt tracks while my head felt warm as exhaustion was finally hitting and I couldn't fight it anymore.

Eddie sat down beside me and pulled me over to him. I didn't bother to fight it. I was too tired. Without caffeine I couldn't make it another hour. I heard him talking to Mike and Henry about something to do with cars and then it was all gibberish as my brain fought between being awake and sleeping.

I snuggled onto Eddie's hardened chest. For something that was equipped to fit on a body builder it was surprisingly warm and comfortable. As his heart beat against my ear, his arm came down around me and I drifted off to sleep. It felt like I had only closed my eyes for a few seconds, but I heard a noise and looked up to see it had been hours. Then I shifted my focus to see the doctor standing in the doorway. I flew out of my chair to get to the doctor. I began babbling incoherent words as I tried to ask how she was and wake up all at the same time.

Everyone gathered as the doctor waited for me to stop slurring words together as if I had had a stroke. Brooklyn grabbed my hand and Mike wrapped an arm around my shoulder. As the doctor began to speak.

"Karen is in recovery. It took a little longer than what we originally thought because there was more in there than what the scan showed. We are awaiting pathology to determine what it is, and you all can see her when we move her back to her room in a few hours."

"Doctor," I shouted and his face said everything without the words, but I had to hear it. "Tell us what you think it is."

"I don't know, we should wait for pathology," he replied, but I knew he was holding something back.

"Doctor," I screamed and pulled his arm as panic overwhelmed me. "You don't know me or my mom, but you should know that I need to know what she is walking into. Her whole life she worked two and sometimes three jobs to give me a life and put a roof over my head. When some boy broke my heart, she was there. When I got a bad grade or skinned my knee, even though she worked all those jobs she was there. When I got a full scholarship to college, she was right there waiting with the acceptance envelope. When I lost my scholarship because of my attendance she was already filing for financial aid for me. You see I don't have a single memory she isn't in. She is my mom, my friend, the cherry to my coke, but most importantly she is my family. My lifeline.

"If you know something, I need you to tell me. Not with absolute certainty because I know pathology has to do that, but I need to know what you know, so I can do burn outs on the track or go rebuild an engine. This way when she wakes up, I have processed it and can be there for her with a smile upon my face. I need to be able to be strong when she sees me, not overwhelmed because we just learned her fate. I need to be able to do this for her as she has done this for me. Please, tell me anything you know."

I was crying by the time I finished talking, it seemed everyone was when I looked around. Henry and Liza were gone, but my true family Brooklyn and Mike were there. Out of the corner of my eye I saw Eddie and even he seemed moved by what I said so I turned back to the doctor in hopes I got through to him.

"When we got her open and the oxygen hit the area you could almost see it spreading. Pathology is going to come back and tell us she has cancer."

"Are you sure?" I asked out of reaction more than a need to know.

"I'm sorry. She will be referred to an oncologist that I have worked with before when one of my patients got sick. She is really good, so try not to over-worry until we hear what she has to say."

Just like that another lifeline was leaving me.

First my job.

Then my money.

Now my family.

"You okay?" Mike asked and I nodded my head, but I wasn't. I couldn't breathe. I couldn't find that constant that kept me standing and strong because she was asleep.

"I just – um – I'm going to get some air. Can you call me when we can see her?" I asked and Mike nodded. I covered my mouth as tears filled my eyes. Eddie called my name and I broke out in a full run out of sight.

Chapter 8

"Don't be mad," a voice called out behind me and usually when someone says don't be mad. I am instantly angry, like a reflex. The air from the roof was crisp and cold, but with him here it turned bitter.

"What the fuck are you doing up here?" I asked as I turned around ready to spit nails.

"I followed you today. I waited and watched in the waiting room. I saw you crying so I just wanted to see if you were okay."

"Go to hell," I shouted and yet instead of listening the asshole took a few steps closer. "I mean it Kurt. Go. The. Fuck. Away!"

I stood up on the roof of the hospital and walked closer to the edge. I knew there was a sidewalk below me that would break my fall and send me to the afterlife, but I was saying a silent prayer it wouldn't get that far.

"I'm not going to hurt you," Kurt spoke softly, and I might have bought it, but he took a few steps closer and then held out his arms. "Come home with me, Kate. Let me help you deal with all of this. Love me, like I love you."

"Get the fuck away!" I screamed. "I swear to God I will jump and die before I let you anywhere near me again."

"You don't mean that," he almost smirked.

"The hell I don't," I said as I struggled to catch my balance when a gust of wind came.

"I'll make you remember who is in charge," Kurt called out as some kind of alpha-gone-wrong episode you expect to find on Skin-Amax.

"Get away from me," I shouted as I wiggled my arms forward to balance my weight when another gust came.

"I'll go because you need some time, but you and I are going to talk about us," Kurt stated defensively with his hands up.

I watched him walk through the door and had to sit down to catch my breath. I knew how to act the part of being a woman they loved for a single night, but Brooklyn was right I had to stop because men like him scare the hell out of me.

Thirty minutes passed and I knew he wasn't coming back, so I sat down and leaned back on my elbows and stared out into the view. It took a little while for my pulse to slow and for my adrenaline to come down, but I wasn't leaving until my mom was awake and I was ready to see her.

The surgery had taken so long that darkness had filled the sky and all that lingered was the famous New York sky line and a collection of stars above me. I had never noticed them before and wondered if it was a sign that I was noticing them now.

I wondered what my mom was dreaming about under the anesthesia. Hopefully it was a great memory like when she taught me to jump rope, or when Mike and her taught me to ride a bike, and not like those memories of the police bringing me home, or when I was an awful teenager and told her she was an embarrassment.

I knew I had been a difficult child, but I had no clue how to make up for it. I didn't even know if she wanted me to, but no matter what the doctors said I would be there for every step.

"Don't jump," Eddie called out from behind me as I came out of my memory lane bubble. I should have been on guard, but his tone was soothing and a little annoying because I didn't want to be bothered.

"What do you want?" I asked without turning to see him.

"The doctor came and told everyone to go home. Your mom isn't waking up like they thought so they are going to move her to ICU for the night. He said you could come back in the morning and visit if she is better."

I stood up and inched my way to the edge of the ledge to look down once more. The people down below were dressed in expensive clothes and trying to make their way back downtown. They would park here and walk so no one saw they were driving a Ford Focus instead of a Dodge Viper. I knew because a week ago I was one of them, and now I didn't know what I was, but I knew things like that didn't matter anymore.

"I used to be one of those people below," I spoke softly. "I cared about what designer I was going to wear and if I packed condoms. I cared about what I wore and not if my mom had been able to eat that day."

"Kate," Eddie called my name, and I shook my head. I didn't want to hear it.

"Can't undo what has already been done."

"Then change what is going to happen," Eddie spoke up and I wanted to smack him for making sense of my thoughts.

"I can't go home," I whispered as I heard footsteps get closer.

"Are you going to be obdurate, and refuse to go home when you are fatigued?" Eddie asked and I nodded my head as the cold wind blew across my face. "Just like the rest of your family," Eddie murmured as he came closer.

"My family is just like me because they made me who I am. Everyone except for Henry, he's not family. I truly don't know him or why he is here."

"I don't really know you, but I know that standing on the edge isn't the answer," Eddie spoke almost mono-toned almost as if he had been trained to talk people down.

"You delivered the message, you can go now," I spoke up as his hand grabbed mine. I watched as he stood up on the edge of the building and looked down with me. "What the hell are you doing?"

"If you fall, I fall," Eddie stated with confidence as if saying it set some kind of a law. I watched his face, he must have been a great poker player because I couldn't tell if he was faking it or not.

"You're insane," I replied. "I'm not going to fall."

"If you jump, I jump," Eddie replied and squeezed my hand to let me know he wasn't leaving.

"You are crazy. If I run are you going to chase me?" I asked and a light grin spread across his face.

"I think I would."

"Why would you think I was suicidal?" I asked and Eddie's grin faded.

"I don't think you are trying to die. I think you are dying to live. Let me take you somewhere to get some food," Eddie spoke as the smell of incoming snow filled the crisp air.

"Don't you get it? I can't leave her. What if she needs me? What if she asks for me? What if she dies?" I instantly cried as I stepped off the edge and onto the blackened roof. Eddie came down with me and wrapped me into his warm embrace.

I held onto him like a life raft in the ocean. I knew my ship was sinking and I knew I needed to save myself, but I just couldn't. I didn't know why this man stayed at the hospital today, but as his arms wrapped around me I didn't want him to be anywhere else.

"Listen to me for a minute," Eddie stated as he pulled me back and forced me to look up at him. He wiped my tears with his thumbs and then his warm minty breath fell on my lips. "She is asleep; healing from surgery. She needs the time to regain her strength and so do you. If you see her like this now, you won't be able to smile. You won't be able to keep the tears away. Trust me when I tell you that taking a few hours to pull yourself together is okay."

"Why do you care?" I asked as his lips hovered over mine. My breathing hitched as I expected him to kiss me, but instead he whispered.

"I'm not sure why I care. I don't know why I want to be here with you. I don't even know you, but something tells me you are my second chance."

"Your second chance?" I asked as his lips moved closer to mine. I shivered with the thought he was going to kiss me, and licked my lips. My heart raced, and my palms grew sweaty. I wanted him to kiss me.

"A second chance to save someone worth saving," Eddie replied and then his warm lips fell on mine.

His kiss surprised me, even though I was expecting it. I had only been kissed hard and fast, but he was soft, soothing, and everything I needed. The way he tilted his head, and wrapped me in his arms left tingles everywhere as all my stress, heartache, and worries all got poured into the kiss. I emptied it onto him and he took it and gave me back warmth, comfort, and care.

I had never been kissed like this before, and wanted more. He didn't push to get inside me. This wasn't a race to get naked. He just allowed me to have the intimacy I needed at a speed that worked for me and everything I was dealing with. I opened and pushed my tongue into his mouth only for him to take control of the kiss back. I needed him to do more. I needed a fix, and holy hell he would do. *Oh fuck, I liked him a lot.*

"I can't," I whispered breathlessly as I pushed him away. I wanted so desperately to deepen the kiss into something else, but men were one of my vices. My body and brain went to war over my need to use him to cope. I knew I wanted to, but I guess I had grown up over night because I didn't want that added stress in the morning. The cons outweighed the pros and I had to push him away.

"Come with me," Eddie stated as he held out his hand and I reluctantly took it. We walked inside the hospital and I was sure he was going to make me leave. I was preparing for a fight to stay, but instead of hitting the stairwell door he took me down the hall. My brain did a complete one-eighty and was no longer wanting to fight him.

A few twists and turns later we were inside some kind of break room. Eddie walked inside the cream colored room and pushed the tables till they were along the walls. The wooden tables had the ugliest orange chairs I had ever seen. They reminded me of prison jumpsuits, which made me a little more anxious because I knew we were not supposed to be in here.

"Don't leave," Eddie whispered and walked out the door. I walked around barely focusing on the environment. Instead, I stared at the clock, as the evilness of time reminded me that we never had enough. The frozen hands didn't move on the clock, but the world around me revolved quickly. In the last twenty-four hours there were lots of moments like this where I struggled to breathe, but I had to force myself to keep going.

"You okay?" Eddie spoke up and I jumped. I hadn't even heard him walk back in the room. I turned to see he had emergency candles lit on the counter and glow sticks standing on the tables.

"I didn't hear you," I admitted and then looked around him to see a familiar face.

"Hi, nurse Kelly," I whispered as her and another nurse rolled in with a large laundry bin filled with blanket and pillows.

"Hello Kate," she replied and looked at Eddie. "You know where these go when you are done. Do not get caught in here."

I looked back at Eddie with confusion as the nurses exited and he took off his leather jacket that fit him in a way the suit and tie didn't. I then looked up at the unmoving clock to see it had been forty minutes since we stepped in here and I began to stare at it. I snapped my attention back to Eddie when he turned off the lights.

"What are you doing?" I ask and Eddie kneeled on the stacks of blankets that made a pad to sleep on, and took my hand. I kneeled down with him and he took off my jacket. I started planning my escape. *I was not having sex with him.*

"Come down here, and lay with me," Eddie spoke softly and I did as he asked. I was still not having sex with him, but something in his voice made me want to do everything he said. I think I know how drug addicts feel because my score was right here, but yet it was agonizing to say no.

"What are we doing down here? Why are you here?" I nervously asked.

"We are not having sex," Eddie replied and I was suddenly disappointed.

"Why did you bring that up?"

"Your heart is racing, and your skin is completely flushed. Your chest and cheeks have a blemish of color that normally comes from being aroused. That would be why I brought it up, but you also stare at the clock and chew on your fingers. This tells me you are impatient, worried, and scared. I know you have a lot going on, so I wanted to ease your mind. Lay down with me and look up."

I did as he asked and saw that we were lying under a skylight. With the lights out I could still see some of the stars and didn't have the cold chill from the wintery air.

"Why are you here?" I asked again in a softened tone as I snuggled against him.

"You didn't want to leave, and I wanted everyone to think I was successful in talking you in to going home and getting some rest so they would go get some rest. It's a win-win."

"You are hiding me?" I asked and he smiled.

"Only for a little while," he replied and I was fine with that. If hiding me meant that Brooklyn and Mike went home and rested, then I was okay with that. Oh hell, Brooklyn was going to think I was sleeping with him because I wasn't at the apartment.

My brain started to race with all things sexual and my breathing sped up. I had zero control, it was all in his hands. I was in his hands. I looked up into his eyes and expected him to kiss me, but instead Eddie tugged me closer to him, and I laid my head on the crook of his shoulder.

"I promise to be a total gentleman tonight. So, if that is what has your pulse up, relax. Take a deep breath, because whatever it is will work itself out."

"I don't know you," I replied with a hint of unease.

"Tell me what you want to know?"

"Are you planning to meet my mom?" I asked and he shook his head.

"I don't know. I don't do this, Kate. I don't get involved with people I don't know. To be completely honest I don't even completely understand why I want to be here with you."

"I'm glad you stayed. It was great for Mike to have another friendly face there," I whispered against his chest as the ticking of the clock drew my attention.

"How do you know Henry Huntington?" He asked and I took a deep breath.

"I don't want to talk about him."

"What do you want to talk about?" Eddie asked as he toyed with the blond strands of my hair. I inhaled him, his scent, his strength, and everything about him. He seemed so strong and sturdy. Like he knew what he wanted from life, but still allowed fate to give him the occasional curve ball.

"I called you an ass-hat," I whispered and I could feel him chuckle quietly.

"You did, and I am still awaiting my apology."

"Keep waiting. I think I like you being around," As soon as the words left my lips I wanted to call them back.

Step one of a twelve step program should be to get rid of the things you are addicted to. I had done the complete opposite and told him to stick around. *I am an idiot.* I would wind up fucking this guy, walking away, and hurting him because something inside me says this whole bonding thing is insane because we just met, but some part of me thought he might actually care.

The silence fell and I wondered what I had done to get someone so sincere in my life at a time when I needed it. No man just did things like this without a reward. Maybe that is what it is, he is waiting for his prize, but walked in at a time where it would be unacceptable to give it to him. Maybe it was from the candle at the church that I lit not only in hopes of saving my mom, but to save me too.

My brain spiraled with the what ifs while he held me tightly and allowed me to go internally insane. I clinched my eyes tight and forced everything swirling in my head to stop. I just wanted to be with him for a while. I hadn't been cuddled by any man this way and wanted to enjoy it.

"Kate," Eddie whispered and I tilted my head up to look at him. "I have a confession. I was the one who swapped our phones."

"Why?"

"Because of a look you had on your face when you were dropping me off."

"What look?"

"I think it was hope." Eddie answered and I knew he had seen it. He had been joking and said he hoped to see me soon. I tried to hide my blush, but he had seen it.

"And today? Why did you stay?"

"It was the lost and frightened look on your face."

"What do you mean?" I asked as clouds started to cover up my stars and light snow fluttered down on the skylight.

"I have a little brother and every time my mom would take us to school she would drop him off at daycare. He would have the same look. He was terrified of the situation, but even more so of asking for help. When I looked at you it was as if you were screaming for someone to make it better without saying a word. I wanted to be there for you. I hope I have helped more than I have been an ass-hat," Eddie spoke sweetly and I realized that he could read right through me.

Most of the men in my life were not around very long. Some call it daddy issues. Some call it poor coping skills. No one ever took the time to learn to read me, but Eddie walked into my life knowing how and that scared me more than anything.

"I am afraid of you," I whispered and Eddie seemed to tense. "You have been amazing today, but you cut through my bullshit to see everything I don't want you to see and that terrifies me."

"Sleep here with me tonight Kate, and tomorrow I may not seem so scary."

Just like he ordered, and I halted all the thoughts and stared at the snow on the glass above me until I fell fast asleep.

Chapter 9

"Kate," Eddie called my name and rolled across the makeshift bed trying to turn into him. "Hey gorgeous," he spoke softly and I reached for him only to realize he wasn't beside me.

"Is it my mom?" I sat straight up as the hair on my neck stood up. Fear enveloped me for no reason. I was going to need a valium here soon.

"No," Eddie knelt down in front of me. "Nurse Kelly is holding a shower for you. They have everything you need. Go get cleaned up, and then go see your mom. She is asking for you."

Eddie started to clean up the candles and pillows as I rose to my feet. I realized that I had actually slept on him and that was a new one for me. I reached over and picked up my phone to see thirty-nine missed calls from an unknown number. I cleared them and looked at my voicemail to see I only had one.

"Hey Eddie," I spoke softly. "In case I don't get a chance to say it. Thank you. I needed a friend without stressing out my family and you stepped up without a second thought. It means a lot more than you realize -," I broke off with tears filling my eyes. *Holy fuck I was in trouble.* I was starting to fall for this guy.

"Kate," Eddie spoke my name as he wrapped me in his arms. Then he pulled back and made me laugh through the tears with a simple question. "Are you always going to call me Eddie?"

I nodded as I pulled back and walked out of the room. I took one last glance over my shoulder to see him watching me and gave him a slight wave in case he wasn't there when I got back. Then I walked down the corridor to see nurse Kelly.

"You are always here," I replied and she nodded.

"I am where I need to be, and where I want to be. Now let's get you cleaned up so your mom can stand you to be near her," she joked, but it took away the hesitation that I felt to follow her.

I pressed play on my voicemail to hear that one message. It was from Kurt. He sounded like he was whispering into the phone.

I can see you snuggled up with that man you were at the diner with. You look so happy, so peaceful as you snuggle into him. I know you are wishing he was me. Wake up Kate, feel me near you and wake up. Come to me on your knees begging for forgiveness.

I nearly threw the phone, but instead I turned on the shower, making a mental note to change my number, and then I scoped out the locker room that Nurse Kelly had brought me into. If Kurt had watched me sleeping last night, there was no way to know if he was still lurking about. I needed to set him straight. I didn't want to be with him, but it would have to wait because my mom was awake and she was my top priority.

"Mom," I whispered as I pushed open her door. I walked inside to see her turned toward Eddie and he was holding her hand.

"I told you she would be right here," Eddie spoke sweetly as he helped her re-adjust to see me.

"Hey mom, how do you feel?" I whispered as I heard a groan slip from my mother's lips. "Do you need anything?"

"Water," her voice cracked and she took a sharp breath when she tried to reach for her light. The beeping on the machine sped up every time she moved or felt pain and it caused the nurses to come in a lot.

"I got it mom, don't hurt yourself."

I took her cup and went and filled it with water from the dispenser at the nurses' station. I questioned whether or not I should tell Eddie about Kurt again, or maybe go see Mark, but I shrugged it off. Kurt was not going to wiggle inside my head, not today.

I grabbed a straw and headed back into the darkened room. I flipped on one of the dimmer lights and walked over to the ghost of a woman that was left in my mother's place.

I fed her through the straw as a nurse came in and took her vitals. I knew my mom had been sick, but it was never this bad. It broke my heart to know that she was in pain and there was nothing I could do to help her.

"Where did the cute guy who brought me flowers go?" My mom asked.

"Behind you," Eddie spoke out.

"He would make a great son in law, Kate. He brought me flowers, but most importantly he is taking care of me for you. You two are destined to be together with my help," she groaned out her words as she shifted around. I think her meds were a little high as she repeated stuff.

"Mom, let's worry about you, and not me," I spoke softly as I pushed the hair away from her face.

"He likes you Kate," my mom murmured. "Don't you Edward?"

"Yes, she is the cherry to my coke," Eddie replied and I laughed. It seemed my mom was working her soda pop girl magic on him as well.

"Aren't you supposed to be at work with your father this morning?" My mom gritted through the pain of moving things around her.

"I am supposed to be, but what is he going to do? Fire me?"

"Kate, you have bills. Just because I am here doesn't mean you need to be here."

"I need to be where you are," I replied with a soft smile and she started shaking her head. "This is not a negotiation, mom." I warned, but her brown eyes shot up at me and I already knew she was going to either guilt me into leaving or soda-pop-girl me.

"Give him a chance to be your dad while the doctors bring me back from the death I feel lingering near me, and change your clothes. I swear you have been wearing that for a week now. You look like hell."

"Mom, I just took a shower and changed into borrowed blue scrubs because we stayed the night. Where would I have gotten scrubs before today?"

"Kate, I think we should have a double wedding," my mom exclaimed and I was sure I was looking at her like she had lost her mind. Her topics of conversation went from one thing to another without rhyme or reason.

"Mom, I think they need to turn down your meds. No one is engaged."

"Kate," Eddie called my name and I looked over at him to see him point over my finger. I turned to see Mike standing in the room in a black suit with a silver tie that had a Ford emblem on a silver pin in the middle. I smiled as I noticed he was holding flowers, balloons, and a little monkey holding a little jewelry box.

"Oh my God," I shouted and started to cry as I stepped out of the way. I watched as Mike dropped to one knee beside her bed and profess years of love to her.

"Karen, you and I have always been together. From neighbors, to co-workers, to friends, and lovers. We have been through love, loss, and this thing called life with each other. We raised this beautiful daughter of ours together. It would make me happy if you could over look my years of stupidity in not asking you sooner, and agreeing to spend our remaining time side by side. Will you marry me?"

Eddie walked over and placed his hands on my shoulders as I cupped my mouth. This was the mom and dad I wanted my whole life and it took her getting sick to show Mike that he needed her as his partner because they were the best part of each other.

My mom shouted "yes," with a rasp and the monitor went off. We were quickly shooed out of the room by the staff. I wrapped my arms around Mike as soon as we were out the door.

"Looks like you are not such a dip shit after all," I murmured in his ear and he laughed.

"Eddie, take my girl here out to your parent's place as soon as you can. I think she will love it."

I didn't know what they were talking about and I didn't care. I had my family, but the dreaded C word still lurked in the back of my mind. My mom may be winning over the love of her life, but she still had another battle in the war.

"I'm going to give you both some time," I spoke as I leaned in and placed a kiss upon Mike's cheek. I needed to get stuff to start my new job tomorrow so that means shopping with Brooklyn tonight.

"Can I see you again?" Eddie asked as Mike stepped back inside the room.

"Eddie," I sighed. "You really don't want to be involved with me. I am a mess. I drink too much. I say fuck a lot when I am mad, like every other word. I like to hit people and use them for sex. I don't even know you, but I know you deserve better than someone who calls you an asshat."

"That might be true," Eddie seemed to tsk to add a little sarcasm to his statement. "You are going to be a handful. I mean *a lot* of work. You don't do what you are told. You are stubborn as an old donkey. You cuss at strangers and you don't like Butterfingers," he finished with a smile. "But Kate, I think you are worth the work."

I could feel my cheeks flame, and for once was speechless. Eddie took my hand and led me to the nurses' station to get my dirty clothes that nurse Kelly had placed in a laundry bag. Then we walked out of the hospital together.

"Well, I guess this is bye," I hesitated unsure if he was planning to give me a ride home or not. He took my long black coat and held it out for me. I turned and placed one arm in each and then turned back to face him while I untucked my hair from the collar.

"No, it's not," he replied and we walked across the street to the parking garage. Then we waited as the valet went to get the car.

"I – um," I started to say, but had no words. I felt like I had known him for years when it had only been a couple days.

"Kate," Eddie stood stoic as his voice deepened. "You are coming with me. Not only do you owe me an apology for the asshat comment, but you ate my Skittles. I think that entitles me to breakfast."

I tried to hide my smile, but the valet pulled up and Eddie walked me over, and opened the passenger door to a white 1957 Cadillac 62.

"Where did you get this?" I asked as I rubbed my hand across the leather on the inside of the door. I loved the square frame on these cars and the decorative pieces that made it seem like they had wings on the end by the trunk. I adored the rounded headlights. My heart raced as I fell in love with the car.

"I have a friend in cardiology who loves older cars," Eddie smile and I corrected him.

"They are not old, merely classic."

"Your chariot awaits," Eddie stated, but I slid myself across the red bench seat to the driver's seat and turned back to look at him.

"Get in, I'm driving," I laughed. "I know how to treat a lady." Then I put the car in gear and Eddie had to dive inside. One day he would learn you cannot trust me with anything with wheels under it.

Chapter 10

"This is not the kind of breakfast I had in mind," I spoke up while Eddie danced in the kitchen from pan to pan. It was almost like he was a one-man orchestra. The sizzling bacon filled the air, while eggs were scrambled, and strawberry and whipped cream covered pancakes dresses the plates. "You are going to make me fat with all that grease," I complained even though I knew I could eat a tub of lard some days, but my mom was still on the back of my mind so my appetite wasn't there.

"You didn't eat yesterday," Eddie told me his observation.

"No, I wasn't hungry. Like I am not hungry now, and am not eating any of that. I would wind up three thousand pounds and six feet under if I ate your cock-cooking."

Eddie pushed the frying pan off the burner and turned everything off. He turned and narrowed his eyes at me.

"What is the real problem here?" Eddie asked and I tried to pretend I didn't know what he meant and my slip of the tongue could be missed. "Go to your room, open your closet, and put on whatever you think makes you look the best. I want to see whatever makes you feel like a beauty queen."

"What?" I asked confused as to why I was getting dressed.

"Do it," Eddie demanded and normally I would have given him a tongue lashing that would make him forget my name and force me into Hail Mary's from the priest, but I kind of wanted to play along.

I walked into my bedroom and looked through my closet. I found my long flowing pink skirt, and my black sweater that was open in the back. I closed my eyes, took a deep breath, and opened my bedroom door to see Eddie leaning up against the door frame looking like dirty sex. Like the kind you know you will love to regret.

"Hello Kate," he welcomed me into the kitchen from my door. He threw a dish towel that was drying his hands over to the island and took my hand to let me inside. "You look beautiful this morning. Your table is waiting."

"What are you doing?" I curiously asked as he walked me over to the kitchen table.

"Treating you like a lady," he replied and I smiled. "You seem to lock up in yourself and need a distraction to let loose."

Then we got to the table and I saw the food I didn't want, but made my mouth water with the aroma sitting across from the table on the counter top. Eddie got a plate for me and placed it on the table and I sat down. Then he walked around behind me and moved my hair off my shoulders and began to rub them.

"Oh God," I called out as he used his fingers and applied pressure as they ran down my spine. My head fell back as he kneaded and massaged every inch of me.

"You are really tense," Eddie whispered in my ear. I moaned and licked my dry lips. Then Eddie stopped and walked to the other chair pulling it away from the table and made it face mine. "Feel a little better?" He asked and I nodded. He seemed pleased with himself and took a fork and tried to feed me a strawberry. I shook my head. "Before I leave you are eating something."

He obviously didn't know me if he thought I was going to do anything I didn't want to do. Eddie's fingers slid into the thigh high slits in my skirt, and inched higher as the strawberry moved closer to my mouth. My heart raced and goosebumps broke out across my body as his fingers went higher on my legs.

"What are you doing?" I asked when he hit the edge of my panties. I couldn't breathe and my brain spiraled with being torn in two different directions.

"Distracting you," Eddie nonchalantly whispered.

"From what?"

"Yourself," he spoke gruffly and placed the strawberry at my lips. Two could play this game. I licked the tip of the berry and then sucked the end of it into my mouth as I leaned forward and placed my hand over his jeans. I copied him and started slowly moving up toward his thigh.

His finger found the edge of my panties and before he could move further I groaned and flicked the strawberry with my tongue. Then I sucked it careful not to pull it from the fork.

Juices flowed out as a little piece broke off into my mouth. When I could feel the fabric stretching from his hardening cock I gripped his leg and moaned as I let a few drops drip down my chin. I watched him gulp as I stopped teasing and moved in quickly to swallow it whole, and then I licked my lips to get the last bit of juice in my mouth.

"Are we done dancing?" I asked as I cocked my eyebrow and gave him a sultry smile.

"You are impossible," he replied, but his stern face changed over to a smile. "It's okay though because I won that round."

"No, you didn't," I called out as I sat back in my chair away from him. "I did because you are going home with blue balls."

"My cock might be angry, but he will get over it because I got you to eat."

I was angry that I didn't see it coming. That I had forgotten why he was here in the first place. Frustration flooded me and I needed somewhere to put it so I threw a strawberry at him.

I watched him flick the strawberry with his tongue before I stood up and turned to walk away, but before I reached the end of the kitchen I felt another strawberry, only this time it hit my shoulder.

I turned and he had a handful and was ready for war. I opened the refrigerator and grabbed the bag of grapes. It was game on.

I loved how he was able to turn my anger into laughter, or delve into the crazy that I carried with me and understand it. I didn't know how Eddie could be so perfect for me, but a sign of an unflawed perfect man, was a sign of bad things to come.

"I think you should go," I shouted bringing the game to a sudden halt.

"No," Eddie replied and sat on the bar stool and put a grape in his mouth.

"We don't know each other and here we are acting like longtime friends, or lovers."

"Are you saying you don't want to be my friend?" Eddie asked with a hint of humor, and I frowned. "Are you saying you don't want to become my lover?" He continued as he walked toward me. "Or is it because you are actually not being bitterly aggressive and having a hint of fun and that scares you."

"I don't want another friend," I lied and swallowed hard. He was getting under my skin and I had to make it stop. I walked to the door and opened it. He grabbed his jacket and walked over standing up against me.

"Ask me to stay," he whispered as our bodies felt the electricity towards each other. It was nothing more than a lack of getting laid and I wasn't doing that with him. "Tell me you are not still scared of me."

I couldn't say a word as Eddie pulled me into his arms. What I wouldn't give to spend just one night with him inside me, but isn't that what every addict wants. Just one more hit, one more fix. Eddie kissed me hard and I grabbed his brown hair and gripped it in my hands.

He moved to my cheek and then kissed just under my ear. I was putty in his hands. He knew he had conquered me, but instead of completing the conquest he leaned over and whispered in my ear before he walked out my door.

"Sometimes when you are given a normal life you don't expect anything extravagant to happen to you and then when it does you can never go back to life as you knew it. You are ruined from what you once knew. That is what happened when I met you. My world ended and real life began. I laughed again, and felt useful. I cared about someone other than myself for the first time in a long time. I don't want to go back to a life of being without the laughter, and you. Don't shut me out Kate, let me in and let me be there for you."

I had stayed up too late with Brooklyn doing Tequila shots, shopping, and explaining why our apartment was covered in fruit. So I took the day off and spent it at the hospital with my mom.

She spent the whole day sleeping or asking where Eddie was because she was going to play matchmaker and make us fall in love. As I got ready to leave for the night I looked over at Mike sleeping on a fold out recliner right beside her and I walked over placing a kiss on her cheek.

"Mom, are you happy?" I asked and she smiled. "How did you know Mike was the one?" I asked and she patted the bed telling me to sit.

"I didn't know he was the one. I loved spending time with him, and we had a relationship that worked for us, but the moment we broke up is the moment I knew, because he told me, and I felt it."

"What do you mean?" I asked because I always lived my life the way I thought she lived hers, but I didn't believe in happily ever after or finding a single person to spend all your time with.

"Kate, when you find a man who thinks you look like a model when you are in sweats. When you find that person who goes out of their way to take your burdens away and make you laugh. When you find the one that you would rather fight with than spend time with anyone else. That is the one, and those are just a couple of signs."

I placed another kiss on her cheek and stood up and walked to the door, but realized she never answered me. I turned back to see Mike awake holding her hand.

"Sorry if we woke you," I called out and blew him a kiss. I turned back and grabbed the hand of the door, but I just couldn't open it.

"What did Mike say? What was it that made you know he was the one?"

My mom sighed and Mike sat up. It seemed like they were more interested into why I wanted the information rather than to give it, but after a few minutes they finally spoke.

"We had agreed that it was moving too fast, and becoming too serious. I was terrified of him, but when we exchanged all our things I picked a fight with him. It was so easy to be angry instead of devastated. I picked a fight over a missing record I said was mine, but was his," my mom rasped out as tears fell from her eyes.

"After listening to your mom yell, and poke me I realized I wanted to fight with her every single day, so I pulled her into my arms and kissed her hard. When I pushed her back she was stunned, speechless. That was the moment I stole her heart," Mike continued as he got my mom a tissue.

"Mike had pushed me away, but all I wanted to do was run to him. When he turned to walk away I wanted to chase him. The moment I met Mike I knew he was different. Things were just so easy with him. He knew what I was thinking the second I thought it. Everything about him was made just for me, but it was too much for me to handle," my mom continued and then stopped to blow her nose which hurt her as she groaned from the pain.

"What did you say?" I asked as that is the one part they had left out.

"When I walked back to my car I looked over the roof and said 'my heart beats begin and end with you. When I leave today you are taking my heart with you. Please don't kill it,' and then your mom ran to me and jumped into my arms for one more last kiss. I opened my car door and heard the sniffles. I turned back to see the tears in her eyes and then I got down on one knee with her hand in mine and asked her to be my best friend," Mike finished and stared at my mom with a longing look.

"What?" I asked wondering how my mom could buy into those lines. That is what men say to get laid, not because they mean them.

"Mike, held my hand on one knee and said 'Karen, I don't know where I would be without you, your support, your friendship, or your love. If I lose your support, I will earn it back. If I lose your friendship I will walk through fire to find that bond again, but I won't us lose the love we found between us, because whatever brought us together only happens once in a lifetime and only to angels," my mom finished the story and pressed her pain medicine button.

I said goodnight and walked out the door with a heavy head as questions swirled on if I was blowing Eddie off too fast.

Chapter 11

The next morning, I was late for work and felt like hell as I had tossed and turned all night thinking of the what ifs. Between starting work for my dad, my mom having cancer, and planning a wedding I didn't have time to think about Eddie, nor did I want to because then I would just want to call him.

I finally crawled out of bed, showered, and stole Brooklyn's clothes. A tight black belted sheath dress. It was sleeveless with a cowl neck and still had tags on it. I ripped the tags off and donned the dress. Brooklyn was going to kill me for taking her new outfit, but at least I would die looking better than I feel.

I refilled my coffee, grabbed a smoke colored cardigan, called for a cab, and then called one of my lifelines.

"Hey Brook," I spoke up as she answered.

"Is Karen okay?" She immediately asked about my mom. I knew she was in court and I was being a tool, but I needed her reassurance.

"She's fine. I need – I – Just tell me I can do this job without killing Henry," I replied. I heard her talking to someone as the phone muffled and then she returned.

"Listen to me, Kate, you can do this, but only if you want to. If you don't feel right about it then tell Henry you don't want to work for him, print out your resume, and go find something else. You can always come work at the law firm."

There it was the proverbial 'If you fuck it up I will fix it.' Brooklyn had been fixing my screw ups for a long time. She had been my partner in crime through high school and college, but something happened to her one day at her dad's parole hearing and she came home different. I still loved her, but felt like she matured overnight and was now a little uptight.

"Thanks, Brook," I stated even though she didn't say anything I wanted to hear.

"Hey, Kate," she stopped me from hanging up. "Don't let him win this round. Don't take any of his shit, and don't let him run you off. I have to get back into court, but I will be at the hospital in a couple hours and will check in then. You got this."

She was right. I had to be the grown up and not let him get to me. I shook off the ill feeling that this was going to end badly, grabbed my things, and headed downstairs to get into my waiting cab.

A half hour later I stared up at the tall skyscraper and knew I couldn't complain about the job I would wind up doing. People came to New York City in search of some acting or modeling dream and wound up waitresses. I however got to be in a place that paid a healthy salary while being under my dad's thumb, and was supposed to act grateful.

"It could always be worse," I whispered to myself.

I paid the cab driver and got out of the car. I walked inside hearing my heels on the black marble floor as everyone else was working and I was forty minutes late. I took in the light grey walls that contrasted with all the black and chrome in the building, if I didn't have to hate him I agree we had the same tastes in decor. I watched people walk past the full glass windows on the sidewalk outside as I rode the escalator to security.

"Hi, I am Kate Huntington. My baby gravy donator is-," I was cut off with a hand to the face.

"We are well aware of who you are Miss Huntington. Your late and your father is in a meeting, if you don't mind waiting I will take you up when he is done," the handsome muscular security guard spoke with disdain for his job.

"I can go up on my own," I scoffed. "I have been here many times. It is not like he doesn't know I am here or I do not know where to go."

He shook his head and pointed to a chair where I sat down and waited. I waited and waited and waited. Four hours I had been waiting while his Chewbacca looking guard stared at my legs, and the Ken doll guard stared at his partner's ass. I had waited long enough. I got up to leave and the hairy security guard came to stop me so I decided to run. I was going to get to Henry and hash this out once and for all.

I started to run and rounded the corner only to run right into a brick wall of tanned muscle in jeans. As my body bounced I fell to the floor and looked up to see familiar brown eyes.

"What the hell are you doing here, Kurt?" I asked as I straightened the bottom of my dress and pulled myself up off the floor.

"I wanted to take you to dinner to celebrate the end of your first day."

"How did you know I worked here?" I asked as my nerves were screaming at me to run like hell.

"I followed you the other morning when you were at the bar with Brooklyn. I called around and found your dad. I just got out of a meeting upstairs. I wanted to ask him for your hand in marriage," he laughed about something as I tried hard to hide the need to call him psycho. "It is kind of funny, your step mom told me to take you and make an honest woman out of you. That is just what I had already planned to do."

"Listen to me carefully. You and I are not together, we are not friends, we are not even acquaintances. I was a stranger who tripped and fell on your cock twice one night and we went our separate ways. Do you understand?"

Kurt grabbed me by the arm, squeezing tightly as he dragged me past the oblivious guard and into an office. The security personnel in there made small talk with Kurt about his last game and then he asked for a moment alone with me.

"Is this because of diner guy? Kurt asked and without hesitation I blurted out words I didn't even know how to put together or what they meant.

"I love him."

"No you don't. He picked you up while you were sad about your mom. Being with him because you feel bad won't last. I'm here and ready to make you feel good all the time."

"You are delirious," I shouted as I crossed my arms. "Spreading my legs for you was the biggest mistake I ever made," my admission was supposed to calm him down, but the way it came out only made him angrier.

"You and I belong together and I am about to remind you of why," Kurt admonished as he unfastened his belt. I said a tiny prayer for a lightning bolt to travel through the seventy-three floors above us just to strike him here and now.

I tried to grab the door, but he back handed me against the wall. I put my hand on my cheek which had flamed with fire. I tried to throw a punch, but he merely shoved me into the water container, knocking it over and pouring water everywhere.

"We will never be together, no matter what you do to me," I screamed as he turned the lock on the door.

"You are mine, Kate! You have always been my whore. Designed by the Gods, made just for my pleasure. You just need to remember who your boss is. Don't you remember? You loved it when I was in charge."

"I love sex, not you," I cried out as he ripped the cowl neck on my dress and shoved me against the wall. I started hitting his chest with my fists, but it didn't seem to faze him.

"Stupid whore, don't talk until your told. Now crawl to me and beg me not to spank you," Kurt growled out and I tried to run for the door as quickly pulled his belt out and whipped it across the bottom of my back. "Count them," he demanded when I shrieked from the pain and hit the ground.

I crawled over to a stack of boxes and started flipping switches and pushing buttons trying to get any of the charging radios to work. When they didn't and he was getting closer I threw one and hit him in the face.

"You need me to remind you of your place, whore," Kurt threw the belt and lunged for me. I leaned back and picked up my legs to keep him at a distance, instead it only broke my heel and pissed him off. "Do as I tell you and you won't have to be punished. I control you, remember."

Kurt grabbed both my arms and flung me across the room. My body bent over a desk as the drawer handled punched into me, and I coughed up blood. I grabbed the heavy duty stapler – that Henry said everyone had to have - and waited.

"I wanted to let go not be controlled," I rebuked as I felt him lift the bottom of my dress. I kicked back, but missed him. He grabbed me by my hair and I screamed, but no one would hear me in here. Everyone was heading home and I was stuck in here with him.

"Tell me you want me," Kurt chided me to give him what he wanted.

"Fuck you!" I replied and he shoved me to my knees with a thigh into my ribs. Then he held me there by my hair as I coughed up more blood and I could feel my body swelling as the aches lingered on.

"Open your mouth whore," Kurt called out and I screamed.

"No, fuck you, let me go!"

He punched me in the jaw and pushed his little cock into my mouth. I choked when slid across my tongue and wanted to puke. With every gag he would pull out and slap me, and we started all over again.

I had to pretended to enjoy it. I stroked him with one hand taking him to the back of my throat and pretending he was someone else to keep the bile down. I had to go to another place in my head to keep it together. I truly thought I might die alone in this room with him.

I thought about everything except what was happening as kept this up charade of wanting to suck him off. As he swelled he threw his head back and let go of my hair.

Then all at once I bite down on his penis and stapled his balls. I heard him scream in a shrill and move away from me as blood rushed down his legs. I stood up on shaky legs wiping the blood from my mouth and replaced the stapler to the desk.

"Don't you ever fucking try to rape another woman or the next time you will see me you will be Bubba's bitch in the penitentiary," I scolded cockily as I headed for the door. I just needed to get the guard to see me and they would call the police.

"Bitch," he screamed and I felt a pang in my head then darkness ensued.

Chapter 12

"It's her own fault," I overheard Liza say. "I mean if you give him the cookie once he is going to want more."

"Liza, not now," I heard Mike say.

"Your presence here is not needed," Brooklyn spoke softly. "You are not her mother, her sister, aunt, cousin, you are nothing in Kate's eyes so take your fake ass plastic double DD breast with the fake spray tan covering up your transparency and walk your happy ass on out of this apartment because when she wakes up you are not going to be what she has to deal with, or the next person to visit a hospital will be you."

I internally smiled because my face hurt when I tried. I loved Brooklyn even more in that moment. I heard Liza scoff and then I heard a door slam. It made me jump, but I kept my eyes shut. I heard a phone making noises, but it wasn't ringing it sounded more like extra loud texting.

"I got the doctors report," Eddie's voice carried into the room, but it echoed like he was in a tunnel and the typing stopped.

"What did they say?" Brooklyn asked and I felt someone take my hand.

"She has a fractured collar bone, and bruising on her lungs. She has a minor concussion and will need to be monitored tonight. You can bring her back to the hospital or keep her in the apartment."

"I'm going to keep her here," Brooklyn spoke up then a new kind of silence came. The one where you know someone is about to say something you don't want to hear.

"Edward," Mike called out. "I need to know did he hurt my baby girl that way."

"No, he didn't rape her," Eddie replied and I felt relief.

"I am trying to get Taylor Cross on the phone as well to find out if they are going to press charges on the stolen car. What do you know from there?" Brooklyn asked.

"The police are on it, but we don't even know where it happened. She walked into the emergency room herself from a car she stole. She was lucid up until the rape kit and then she just blacked out. They are telling me she is the lucky one that she survived it, and that Kurt might not ever use his equipment again."

"That's my girl," Mike happily retorted. "She has never been one to go down without a fight."

"Who caught the case?" Brooklyn asked.

"Richard Sanchez, out of the 11th precinct."

"She would be more comfortable with detective Mark Stone. We all went to school together so he will know how to handle her smartassness. I'm going to see if Taylor has any favors he can pull and I will owe him."

"I feel responsible," Eddie said out loud and it forced me to make my eye lids cooperate. The room was bright, and I looked to see I was in my room in my own bed, but everything was blurry and it hurt my head.

"Why?" Brooklyn asked the same question I wanted to know.

"He bothered her the other night and I wrote it off as him being drunk with a crush on her."

"You couldn't have possibly known," Mike spoke up and then the conversation seemed to fade and the room went dark.

I opened my eyes to see a darkened room. I looked beside me and Brooklyn was curled up next to me. I tried to turn into her, but my shoulder told me I wasn't putting any weight on it. I was strapped in some kind of brace that held my shoulders back. My head hurt like hell and I needed to get up to pee, but my arm wouldn't let me.

"Brook," I whispered and she sighed. I said her name again and she opened her eyes.

"Hey Kate," she said as if she hadn't seen me for a while. "How do you feel?"

"I can't get up," I whimpered with a dry throat. "I really have to pee."

Brooklyn got up and walked around to my side of the bed and helped me up. She kept a hand on me the whole way to the bathroom. My head felt heavy like it could fall off my neck if I didn't balance it perfectly. I noticed I was in an extra-large t-shirt and smelled like a man. It made me gag.

"What happened?" I asked as I saw the bruises under the bathroom light. Brook didn't have to answer because I already knew. It came flooding back to me like a rerun on the fox network.

"Kurt has been arrested and charged with assault and battery, and attempted rape. They don't expect him to make bail. Taylor and I talked yesterday and the state is not going to press charges on you for the theft of a car if you agree to pay the money to get the blood detailed out of the seat.

"Why would they charge me? I'm a victim," I spoke loudly enough that my brain felt like it was going to splatter as I peed into the toilet.

"You damn near bit his penis off. You stapled his balls – The staple had to be surgically removed as the leg on it went nearly an inch inside his testicle. That alone would have been impressive, but then you stole a car and dropped him off with the word rapist written in lipstick across his ass two blocks from the hospital in Central Park at night."

I busted out laughing and it hurt. I cried, and giggled all at once. I shook my head, I was capable of a lot of things and remember the staple, but not the car or the park.

"You don't remember any of that?" Brooklyn asked with concern etching her face.

"I remember waiting all day. Henry kept me down there for hours. Then Kurt was there. I remember him wanting to take me to dinner, and -," I stopped. I couldn't say out loud what he did.

I wiped and Brooklyn helped me stand back up. I heard a whistle calling and started slowly walking out to go into the kitchen. I rounded the wall to see Mike and Eddie playing some card game while Taylor Cross boiled tea.

I hated the smug District Attorney, with his perfect black hair, his flawless tan skin and bright white teeth. His exemplary eyes that screamed guilty to everyone who looked at them. *Why couldn't he be blessed with acne, or a lisp?*

"Why are you here?" I asked and Taylor smiled. I didn't like him when he tried my case and I sure as hell wasn't smiling back at him now.

"We were all playing cards, taking shifts with you, and wondering if sleeping beauty was going to wake up."

I looked at Brooklyn and she nodded as she steered me over to one of the navy blue chairs that sat across from the couch. Then Brooklyn went and sat on the loveseat and leaned up to hold my hand.

"What is this an intervention?" I asked as I cleared my dry throat and everyone looked around the room. "I haven't known Eddie long enough for him to be here if that is what it is."

"May I call you Kate?" Taylor asked and my professionalism went out the window.

"You can call me whatever you want from your cell phone as you get in your cab to leave."

"Kate, Taylor will be trying Kurt as a favor to me. I need you to cooperate. We know mostly everything, but we have a few questions."

"Fine," I sighed and sat back in the chair only to wince at the pain. Brooklyn made me tea and brought me pain pills.

"Do you remember where you stole the car?" Taylor asked and I shook my head. "Do you remember how you knocked Kurt unconscious or loaded his two hundred and ten pounds of dead weight into the back of a car?"

I shook my head, but I got this stomach sinking feeling they knew more than I did. Especially with Taylors tone.

"Do you remember saying no?" I nodded. "Do you remember where this happened?" I looked over at Eddie and then at Mike. I shook my head with the lie. Knowing Mike he would blame Henry and kill him for leaving me in that position. "Will you be all right working with Detective Stone on this, or would you like me to have them assign you a female detective?"

"I can work with Mark. He has seen me in worse shape than this."

"Kate, I need you to think really hard. Was there anyone else with you? Someone who helped you get to the hospital? Anyone tell you not to talk about what happened?"

Bells went off in my head and made it hurt even more. I wasn't raped because I hadn't been alone. I scrunched my swollen face as I tried like hell to remember. My head ached, but there was nothing there. Just glimpses into what he made me do.

"Kate," Eddie spoke softly and I jumped when his hands laid on my knees. I felt the hot tears strolling down my face as I looked into his eyes. I was angry. So very bitter, and even Eddie's bedroom eyes couldn't make this go away. No joke was going to fix this.

A distraction was useless because now the video feed was playing over and over in my head. The way he grabbed my hair, and forced me to let him into my mouth. The way he repeatedly hurt me when I stood up for myself.

"Kate," Mike called out and I flinched as they all backed away. I was stuck in my head replaying it over and over again. I couldn't get it out. I couldn't make it stop.

"Kate, listen to me," Brooklyn yelled through my vision, but I couldn't see her. All I could see was Kurt. Then I felt my body turned to ice, and I shrieked. I closed my eyes tightly as I covered my head. "Kate!" Brooklyn screamed and I looked up to see I was in the shower. I was laying in the tub with cold ice water pouring down on me. "You were tearing your own skin off," Brooklyn moved slowly toward me and showed me where I had tried to claw the skin off where he had left the first bruise.

"Brooklyn," Taylor called out and she turned off the water. Then she stepped out of the room I was left with Eddie in the bathroom with his back to me.

"I'm - I'm so sorry," I cried as I shivered. I wanted him to turn around, to hold me, to make it better, but we both knew I would never be the same if he did. That everything would be lost.

"It is not your fault."

"I didn't - I wasn't," I sobbed. "I'm not a whore."

Eddie started to talk, but I couldn't hear anything he had to say. I wasn't in a place to listen.

"I'm a soda pop girl," I bawled into the cold tub. "I'm a tasty treat," I wailed as the reality of my choices came to life. "I am not a slut!"

Brooklyn barreled back into the room and I kept telling her everyone over and over again. It was my life and my choice to be who I was and I still made no apologies for it. I wasn't a saint, but I wasn't a sinner who deserved what happened.

"You said no," Brooklyn said sternly. "No means no. You didn't do anything wrong! If you believe anything I ever say, you need to believe that."

Chapter 13

The weeks came and went. Henry paid my rent in full, and I now had a driver to take me to my mom's chemo appointments and to the garage. Henry had agreed to leave it open until I didn't have to wear a brace because it would lower moral at the company to wear it in the office.

Seemed that his female staff wanted more security after what happened and Henry felt like he had paid enough so I was hidden, tucked away like I didn't exist.

"How is my favorite daughter?" Mike asked. He and my mom got married right after the incident with Kurt. My mom thought it would be a way for me to find my smile, and I did. I looked over at the calendar and grinned when I saw it had been exactly a month.

"I'm really good dad," I said sweetly and my attention turned to the red 1966 Ford Mustang

Fastback sitting in the back of the garage. "Why is that one back here?" I asked as I hadn't seen Eddie since the morning after the incident.

"He broke the fan blade," Mike stated with a shake of his head. "Someone should take the time to talk to him so he will stop breaking the cars in hopes of seeing you."

I ignored the comment and walked over to the car. I ran my fingers across the hood, but it didn't carry the same feeling anymore. I was broken and I didn't know how to get my sass back.

"Hey Mike," I called out and he looked around the hood of an Oldsmobile from me. "I'm gonna fix it and take it to the track."

Mike merely smiled as I pulled my hair back from my face and I leaned over the hood. Shorter pieces of my hair fell forward out of the band. A reminder of what had happened. When they arrested him he had pieces of my hair tightly wound in his hand.

I had to shake the thought from my mind, and get to work on this car. Eddie and I knew each other for a few days. It wasn't a lifetime, even though it felt like one. It wasn't love, even though I fought myself hourly to not call him. He was a drug of choice I never tried, but had wanted to.

There was no more one night stands. No more partying or going to the club. I got up showered, drank coffee, went to work, returned home, had dinner, and went to bed. There was constantly someone with me courtesy of my sperm donor. I didn't know if it was to keep me safe, or to keep me from biting anymore cocks.

"Kate," Mike called over my shoulder. "You should drive it over to him and let him know that you are okay when you get it done."

"And let Daddy dearest find out I went somewhere without my driver who looks like he could be broken in half by a five-year-old," I put as much sarcasm into that as I could muster.

"Kate, the man is worried," Mike kept on.

"Tell him to read People Magazine if he wants a good story. I'll be featured in the life's most boring category next month."

"Sometimes Kate, you are as stubborn as your mother," Mike said in passing, but it made me grin. A true smile. Something I struggled with often.

A few hours later, I had fixed the Fastback and had driven her to the race track. With one hand on the wheel and one on the shifter I was ready. I closed my eyes and put everything out of my head. Brooklyn was moving out in a few weeks, and in a week I would no longer be in a brace. My mom was doing better, but I felt like the doctors were withholding information. Kurt was offered a plea deal to keep me from having to see him again, but Taylor didn't offer him much. I think it was six months off the maximum sentence. Kurt still had not accepted it.

All of these things combined led me to this race track where I could drive faster than my problems could fly. I opened my eyes and turned on my Ipod and placed the buds in my ear because you couldn't get Black Sabbath on eight track, and then tightened my seat belt.

I pulled up a little closer to the line and then waited for the other driver to get off the track. Once he pulled out I let off the clutch and pressed the gas to the floor. The tires burned as the car jumped forward and I quickly slammed it into second and then third. Within two minutes I was clearing the governor at eighty-five miles an hour. It wasn't nearly fast enough, but being able to race this car was everything to me.

Even racing I couldn't put the changes behind me.

The wind in my hair.

The thrill of the road.

The sound of the engine purring.

And the way the car just seemed to know what I was thinking made it all worth it, and I used to love it. I couldn't get enough and now I wondered how much gas I was wasting.

I hugged the curve on the tenth lap a little too tight and it caused me to slam on the brakes. I knew better, it was something you never do. Always let off the gas, and downshift I chastised myself. I saw the smoke as the car came to a stop and I lunged out as the track employees came running out with fire extinguishers.

"I am such an idiot," I chided myself as I watched his brake pads go up in flames, and ruin the paint on the wheel wells.

I called my driver, and a tow truck and let them come and get us both. I didn't have the money to fix the damage and those parts are hard to come by. It would have been no big deal if only the pads needed replacing, but with cars that old anything the fire got near would have to go. Which meant I had to call Henry and ask for the money.

"Dad," I responded with my best ass kissing voice. "I need to borrow about ten thousand dollars."

I explained the whole thing to him and he agreed to pay, if I started working for him tomorrow. I agreed with no smart ass comment. No quirky quip.

The verdict was in and I was found: Broken beyond repair.

I knew I was going to have to face Eddie and explain the damages to the car. So I picked up my phone and sent him a text. Then I dialed Mike, he was going to be disappointed, but he wouldn't be any harder on me than I was on myself.

I found myself waiting for Eddie at an old park that sat down by the river. I sat in the swing and closed my eyes. Nothing says you love New York City like breathing in the toxins from the freighters down by the port, and I loved every bit of it.

"Hi," Eddie called out from behind me. I turned and saw he was like twenty feet away. "I didn't want to sneak up on you while you are getting high on tanker diesel," he joked, but I just stared at this man who I knew I wanted, but couldn't have.

"Hi, Eddie," I called back and pulled the swing beside me to give to him. "Want to swing with me?"

"How about I push you?" He responded and I noticed he was in a charcoal suit with a lilac tie. He must have come straight from work to see me. He acted weird, like I was fragile and it made me ask myself, was I?

"I broke your car," I blurted out as he pulled my swing back, and then he slowly let me forward then he sat in the swing beside me. He turned and slowly put his hands on my knees to turn me. "Fuck Eddie, I won't break," I replied as I watched him move in slow motion.

"I wouldn't know. I thought we were on a path to be friends or something and then when something bad happens to you and I want to be there for you, you cut me out of your life."

I pushed his hands away, stood up, and paced in the sand.

"We were moving too far or too fast. I can't explain it, but staying away from me is the best thing you can do. When I run -," Eddie cut me off as he stood up and grabbed my head in his hands and kissed me hard and fast.

His tongue licked my lip and I opened to let him in. He was the one man I needed and wouldn't let myself to have. I wanted to climb on him and drive his stick into me. I pulled away breathlessly resting my forehead on his chest.

"When you run, Kate, I'm going to chase you."

"Chase me?" I asked as I looked back up. "Am I a game of cat and mouse? Something that has a finish line?" I knew I was blowing things out of proportion, but he had crossed my invisible safety zone area into my feelings. I didn't want to like him. I didn't want to miss him, but I did.

"No, Kate, that is not what I meant," Eddie tried to defend himself, but I wasn't going to let him.

"What did you mean?"

"Kate, don't be difficult -," he spoke softly as I got louder.

"Now I'm fucking difficult?"

"What is your problem?" Eddie asked and without a filter my words came tumbling out.

"With Kurt I could defend myself because it was all physical, but with you I can't. I like you and I hate that I like you. I came to depend on you, but you weren't there when I needed you the most."

Eddie took a step back and ran his fingers through his brown hair. He took a deep breath and talked calmly towards me.

"You wouldn't let me be there. I wanted to be, but you put up your orange traffic cones that said all roads to you were blocked. I like you Kate, and I thought maybe we could be really good friends, or if you dropped the no dating rule we could go out and have fun, but no one is ever going to make you happy when you push everyone away like this."

"I'm sorry," I mouthed silently as I saw Eddie's frustrations shine through.

"Stop being sorry, Kate, just let me in or let me hate you."

"Let me take you to see the car, and then you can decide if you hate me."

Chapter 14

My driver drove out to the garage to see the lights out and chains on the outer bay doors. Then a giant sign said closed.

"You okay?" Eddie asked as we slowed down to a crawl as the car crept up the gravel drive.

"Yea. Just wondering where my dad is," I lied as my lip quivered on Eddie.

The giant orange letters that spelled closed, punched me in the gut and stole the air in my lungs. I didn't understand why you can have every thought in your head, and you are unaffected, but when you read them in a book, on paper, or on a giant sign they become real. I knew what Henry was going to do, but I somehow denied it until now.

"I can't believe my dad closed it up now that I am supposed to work for him. It wasn't supposed to happen this fast," I mumbled out loud to myself.

"Why would your dad close up his own shop when you are supposed to work with him," Eddie stated his confusion.

"Mike is not my real dad. Henry Huntington was the man who splewged in my mom. Although there is still some debate as to whether or not I am actually his in my opinion. I am more inclined to believe the star dust theory."

"What star dust theory?" Eddie asked and I put the divider up between us and my driver who also moonlighted as a snitch to Henry.

"There is this theory that I was once a bright star. Like the north star, you know the ones you can't help but see because they don't give you a choice," I explained and Eddie smiled. "The theory says that when I filled up with wishes I shot across the atmosphere as my gas escaped and landed in the ocean, but I never fully burnt out. A amoeba found me and carried me near the shore giving me time to recharge my energy. When I got to shore I adapted and crawled out of the ocean taking on the first thing I saw, a baby girl, and then my mom found me and kept me."

"So, your theory is you were a shiny ball of gas who farted and morphed into a baby?" Eddie asked with both humor and disbelief all over his face while he fought back the laughter.

"Something like that, although it is more romantic when I tell it. Truth be told any theory is better than him being my mom's easy bake oven's batter."

As I looked at the chains on the bay doors and no trespassing signs that are all over the garage. I got out of the car and walked around the building. I noticed one of the upper windows was still cranked out.

I went back and told my driver I was about to give a blow job and asked him to go get me Jolly Ranchers or peppermints. He looked at me like I was a weirdo, but went anyway. I made a mental note to find out if he was gay.

I turned back to Eddie on the side of the garage.

"Eddie can you give me a boost?" I asked and his face fell.

"The name is Mr. Wellington, Edward, or Sir."

"Sure Eddie whatever you say," I responded waving my hand to tell him to boost me. "You and I both know I will never call you anything, but Eddie."

"I should spank you every time you get my name wrong. I hate that," he stated and I had to smile that the one thing we had in common was people getting our names right. "I have known you all of a couple months and you already want me to commit a crime with you." Eddie tried to talk with a straight face, but he failed to hide the laughter as his smile shined through. "What is in it for me?"

"I have Skittles," I called out and he chuckled. "I will give you all the nasty green apple ones."

"I want the red ones, not the green. Everyone knows they should have stayed with lime and not apple," Eddie negotiated right back to me.

"Half of the red, and I will give you five of each of the others," I countered.

"How about half the red, and dinner," Eddie challenged.

"The kind we go out for or the kind where I cook and we go to the emergency room with food poisoning?"

"Out, definitely the kind we go out for," Eddie laughed out his words. "I pick when and you pick where," Eddie added and I smiled. It would be a first for me if I got to pick where I went to dinner with a man.

"Not a date," I spoke up and Eddie smirked.

"Not a date, more like a get to know you therapy session with food. I don't think you will get to know me or vice versa while we are breaking the law, do you?"

"You are seriously the best ever," I chuckled as he put his back up against the garage and folded his hands. I took off my shoes and climbed into his waiting hands.

Eddie lifted me up to the window and I slid inside the opening. I stepped down on my tip toes onto a bookcase of tools and slid down onto boxes before hitting the concrete floor. The lights were off and the room was ominous. There were still five cars inside waiting to be fixed. All the tools were still out as if Mike had just taken the afternoon off.

"You okay?" Eddie shouted and I went to the alarm and turned it off before it called the police from the motion detector. The bay doors were chained from the inside and the outside. It was a bit overkill, but there was a lot of money sitting in here.

"Hang on," I shouted back and started trying each door. They were all locked up tight. I pushed a giant black tool case and unlocked a hinge on the bottom of the garage and lifted the rectangle shaped piece of metal. "You have to crawl in this way."

Eddie slid on his belly to get inside, and I helped him stand back up as he gave me the look that said he had a million questions.

"When I was a teenager and needed to get away I would come down here. One month when my mom couldn't pay the rent because she had gotten pneumonia and taken a couple days off work I came down here and stole some stuff to sell. The next weekend I came back to return some of the stuff, but Mike's mean partner came in after me and worked through the night. I couldn't do anything. I couldn't get caught and put that stress on my mom, so I stayed all night in the trunk of a 1949 Plymouth. When I woke up there was an alarm, and all the doors were bolted.

"I used the welding tools to cut a person sized doggy door and even added the hinges so it was not noticeable and just swung as I came in and out. Mike figured it out and busted me for it. My punishment was to come and work with him on the cars. I loved being down here working on them, and being with Mike. He is the dad I wish I had. The added plus was it helped my mom pay rent because Mike would pay me to help him."

Eddie handed me my shoes to put back on, but I merely sat them on the shelf while Eddie walked over to his Fastback and climbed inside. He let his head fall back and breathed in the smell of old leather.

"You are an enigma," Eddie spoke softly and I walked towards him in question. "You are absolutely stunning, and yet with your manicure and perfectly styled clothes and hair you would rather be in a dirty garage being a tomboy. I don't think I have met anyone like you."

"I cuss like a sailor, drink like a fish, fuck like a whore, and yet I know how to play the part of acting like a grown up when I have to. I don't think that makes me different. It just means I am versatile."

He patted the seat and I walked to the passenger door and opened it to climb inside.

"You ever done anything you wish you could take back?" I asked and he nodded.

"My parents died in a car accident when I was in college. They were headed home from visiting me. There was this girl and I didn't want to be bothered. So, I yelled at my dad in the quad for all to see telling him he was an embarrassment to the family. I told my mother she was just as bad to have settled for him. I said some really bad things. Those are the last things I ever said to them. They told the paramedics they loved me and forgave me. They didn't want me to live with it on my conscience, but if I could that would be the one thing I would change. What about you?"

"I wish I could take back the day of my college graduation. That was the day my mom decided to find my dad. Two years later, I met the trailer trash and his troll who he was merely engaged to. I would definitely change that."

"That the only thing?" Eddie pried and I swear he read right through me to know that I didn't really care if I changed that or not. I took a deep breath and chose to go with honesty when everything in my body said to lie to him.

"I once slept with a married man," I mumbled under my breath. "I didn't know he was married. His wife was away on a business trip and I was lonely, he was lonely. I was young so I thought we had something real something shiny and new, but instead it was like the fake gold that turns your finger green."

"What happened?" Eddie asked and I swallowed hard. I hadn't talked about this in a really long time. Since before college.

"His wife came home and he came clean. She filed for divorce and took their daughter. It was brutal. They both loved each other and were both hurt by what happened, and when they finally let go of the anger and resentment they got back together, but their daughter, this little blond thing that reminded me of myself was never the same."

"That can be hell on a kid, and seems like you were a child then too. Why is that the one thing you would change, when it helped them reconcile?"

"Because it is the only time I ever felt ashamed for the way I lived. I have never seen a guy twice since then unless it was just in passing. Call it daddy issues or whatever, but my mom made it on her own and so will I."

"You know you don't have to live your life alone, right?" Eddie asked as I sat beside him and toyed with my fingers to keep my emotions off my face from his last question. Silence grew with my refusal to answer. I needed to change the subject.

"I'm not a crier," I fumbled the words out without a point to them. Eddie turned to look at me. "I never cry, well almost, I don't cry unless it is one of my lifelines."

His brows furrowed, and I knew I wasn't making much sense. I had gone from talking about the one regret I had to my lifelines. I was sure this guy was going to get whiplash riding my crazy train.

"I broke your car driving faster than my own problems. I mean it's not totaled or anything. I merely caught the undercarriage and wheel wells on fire."

Eddie reached over and took my hand and placed it in his. He had this way about him that was like he was a therapist. When he was silent I wanted to tell him anything he wanted to hear to get a reaction and my filter was still busted so I blurted it all out.

"Brooklyn is moving out. She hasn't said it yet, but she took this new job I have to pretend I don't know about, and when she leaves I will have lost her. She will want to join the grown-ups where people don't say what they think, they drink in moderation, and fun is what they reminisce about or they tell their kids to go do it.

"I don't like my sperm-dad's wife because she is a human floatation device with a brain the size of a broken peanut. He isn't much better as he lost his balls to her so he fires people she wants gone to avoid letting them have their retirement. I hate the idea of working for him, but my mom took care of me and I want to help take care of her medical bills now that he has fired Mike-," I got cut off.

"Kate," Eddie whispered and I looked up at him realizing that my focus had dropped to my feet. "You don't always have to be strong. You should tell people how you feel so they can react accordingly."

"Tell me about you. I feel cut open, and yet I know nothing about you," I whispered and Eddie smirked.

"I'm old, fat, smelly, and poor," Eddie chuckled as he loosened his tie.

"Tell me something I might believe," I retorted.

"I'm an inch and a half and I cum real fast," he stated with too much enthusiasm hoping I would buy it.

"I want to sell you beach front property off the coast of Arizona."

The tension in the air from me unloading my info had evaporated. It felt like before Kurt happened. It was so easy to just tell him my problems, get it off my chest, and then he would make it better. He was able to distract me in just a few sentences where life didn't seem so overbearing. *Ah, shit... I was head over heels for this guy.*

I took my hand back quickly and Eddie's brown bedroom eyes glanced up at me and I knew it to be true. How the hell could I like him when I kept myself guarded?

"I think we should leave," I stated as I climbed out of the Mustang. I shut the door and a red light flickered on the wall. When I looked away from it Eddie was right beside me.

"What's wrong?" He asked and I couldn't tell him I liked him. Not again. That would be the worst thing to do. "Is it because you still don't know me?" He asked and I nodded the lie. I knew him.

I knew he was husband material, and would have two point five kids. He would continue to work directly under Henry for another five to ten years and then step out and start his own company. Something he could pass down to his kids. Then he would retire to the only penis shaped state, Florida, and spend his days getting denture free oral at the retirement village.

"I graduated from high school at sixteen with honors, and got a scholarship to Western Carolina University where I majored in Emergency Medicine. I then worked as a EMT as I attended Harvard and graduated with a Master's in Business Administration. Henry came to me before I graduated and offered me a job in his firm. He paid off my Harvard loans and I am contracted to stay with him until I have paid it back."

I walked across the car and stood there in front of Eddie and took his hand in mine.

"Seems we are both hostages to Henry," I joked, but his face was serious. "What would you do if you had freedom?" I asked and he answered without a second thought.

"I would be a paramedic. I want to help people live, not build portfolios and run companies. I once thought about building up my bank account and buying my contract out, but then everyone who I have helped financially would be lost in Henry's mediocre system."

Chapter 15

My body took control as my heart warmed to his answer. I pulled on his lilac tie, bringing him down to me. I placed my lips on his and fireworks exploded in my veins as the blood rushed through excessively fast. I slowly wrapped my arms around his head as he kissed me back. I felt his arms tighten around me as he lifted me off the ground and laid me on the hood of the Mustang.

I was going to be ruined for every man with a kiss like his. It was soft and warm like hot velvet, it kept me yearning for more, like a drug. When I wrapped my legs around him and pulled his tighter to me. I felt him harden through his suit, and without warning my clit hardened and pulsated. I could feel the wetness under my panties grow as I realized I was in my own fantasy. It wasn't a vineyard, but who the hell cared when he kissed like that.

Then the flood of ice came pouring down my spine. I couldn't do this. I went from wanting him to climb on top of me to fighting him to get off.

"Kate," Eddie said calmly "Kate, breathe with me," he stated and I felt his chest. I breathed in when he breathed out. After a few moments we were in sync and I felt foolish for my overreaction.

"Eddie," I whispered into his ear. "I'm sorry. I want to, but-,"

"Shhh," Eddie breathed into my ear and goosebumps flooded my shin. Tingles traveled back down my spine and it was like the panic attack didn't happen. "We aren't going to do anything you don't want to do."

"I need you to make me," I tried to explain., and saw his hesitation. I reached down and unbuckled his pants.

"Kate," he growled in frustration. "You aren't ready and I can't force any woman to do that."

"Please," I begged as tears filled my eyes.

"I can't force you."

Then I sobbed as Eddie held me close.

"Kate, tell me what is going on in your head," Eddie spoke sweetly as he held me tight.

"I can't stop freaking out, but I want to. I need to do this. I need to move past this. He can't win this part of my life."

I tried to explain, but he didn't understand. Maybe I needed a victims support group, but I wasn't raped, at least not in the sense that he penetrated something other than my mouth. I needed to get Eddie to understand that I needed him to do this for me because there was no other man that I trusted enough and felt this way about that would get me over the hump.

"Please, Eddie," I begged as tears fell from my face. "I need it to be you. I need you to make me so I can have this part of my life back."

"Kate, I want to, but I can't force you to. I can do a lot of things, but when you say no or you get upset I stop."

"Then we will just have to breathe together when it happens," I whispered as I unzipped his pants. I could still see hesitation in his eyes. I pushed him up and unzipped my own jeans and pushed them down my legs. I then pulled my sweater off and waited there for him to judge my body, but his eyes never left mine.

"You sure you want to do this?" Eddie asked and I nodded.

"Foreplay?" Eddie asked, but I shook my head. I didn't want to second guess myself. I didn't want to have time to think.

Eddie pulled a condom from his wallet and I took it and tore it open with my teeth. I pulled his pants down never letting my eyes drop from his. Then I pinched the tip of the condom and let it roll down his long hard cock. Once he was sheathed I looked down at him in my hands. Holy hell, he was definitely going to be able to hit all the right spots with that.

"Kate, I can't make you," Eddie started, but I saw him fumbling his words. "I have never –

where the girl was in control, but I think that is what you need."

"What?" I asked as I unhooked my bra and let it fall to the floor.

"When I am making all the decisions like now your shaking, but when you had control of the condom you didn't. I think you need to be in control for this, not to be forced."

I pulled my white panties to the ground and stood naked before him as his pants around his ankles limited his movements. I pushed his jacket off, took off his tie, and unbuttoned his shirt. I swallowed hard when I pushed it off of his shoulders. I had been right; this man spends a lot of hours at the gym. I traced his abs till I got to the V in his stomach and then I picked up his hands and placed them around me.

"I don't know what to do next," I whispered as a million thoughts flooded me.

"Stop thinking and feel," Eddie said and then his lips landed on mine. His tongue grazed my bottom lip begging for entry and I let him in. I deepened the kiss and wrapped my one arm around his neck while the one that was still sore from the injury wrapped around his chest.

Eddie walked me the two steps backward and laid me back on the hood of the Fastback. He took control for a minute as he bit the place where my shoulder and neck meet. I moaned and he stopped pushing forward.

He moved his head down to my breast and sucked my pale nipple into his mouth. My back bowed up off the car and memories flashed into my mind. I couldn't breathe as the video feed began in my head.

"Breathe with me," Eddie repeated through the montage in my brain. I focused on hearing his breath and shoved Kurt back into a box and stored it away under never remember in my memory bank.

"Can you -," I started when my breathing was fast, but not erratic. "Will you-," I struggled with the words. My brain picked a hell of a time to turn my filter on. I reached down and grabbed his staff and moved it toward my entrance.

"Be sure you want to do this," Eddie stated and I placed my hands on his shoulders and stared at that one sliver of green in his eyes. I nodded my head and let out a deep breath I had been holding.

I felt him at my entrance, but he was as unsure of this as I was. I didn't want to freak out and he didn't want me to either. I closed my eyes for a moment and cleared my head of nothing but Eddie and I.

"This shouldn't bother me. I mean he didn't rape me, so this should be fine."

"Kate, be sure cause we can stop at any point," Eddie confidently stated as if he was in complete control of himself, but I saw the sweat building up when he looked at me. He wanted me like I wanted him.

"Go slow," I groaned as I felt him push into me. He was so slow that my nerve endings danced to life with anticipation while my skin stretched to accommodate him.

"This feels better than some orgasms I've had," I said out loud on accident. The look of pride that crossed Eddie's face was pure joy for me. I gripped his arms as he pushed further in. Once he was in to the hilt he held perfectly still and allowed me to adjust to him.

"I need to be on top," I cried out as I started to freak out. Eddie lifted me off the car and took baby steps to a Cadillac, and opened the back door. He sat on the edge and leaned in so he didn't hit the door frame and then he slid across the bench seat. "You didn't want to fuck in the Mustang?" I asked and he laughed.

"No, not yet," he replied and I smiled. He was laying beneath me in the back seat of a stranger's car, and the power was now in my hands. I lifted myself up and glided back down a few times as the thrill and excitement re-flooded my veins.

I moved up and down, front to back grazing my clit across his skin from time to time. I grabbed his hands and placed them on my hips. He helped me find the rhythm we both moaned at, and I rode him.

"Fuck," Eddie called out when I tightened down on him and heard the intake of air in his teeth as I did it again. Eddie sat up and wrapped his arm around my waist as he sucked my nipple into his mouth again.

I felt like I was on fire, and moving toward an explosion as tension built up. This seemed more intimate than any other tryst I had ever had. He couldn't keep from touching, or kissing me and the intensity grew stronger as I clawed at him unable to stop myself.

His other hand slid in between us and spread open my folds to find my throbbing clit. His finger moved in a circular pattern as my head fell back and I groaned. I stopped riding as the feeling got too intense, but neither of us were done. I wanted him without having to always be in control, and I think he knew because Eddie slid us back out of the car and carried me away from the car with kisses on my neck and shoulder.

He moved me to the wall and pinned me to it. I should have flipped out, but didn't all thoughts of Kurt were on some other dimension while Eddie was inside me. He kept his hands under my knees. I sunk just low enough for his wide head to hit that rough patch behind my pelvic bone and make me chant his name.

"Fuck," Eddie called out as I screamed. I grabbed his face and kissed him deeply. I had never felt like this. I desperately tried to make us one as I tightened down on him. I needed him more than the desert needs rain.

I heard sirens in the distance and looked to see a new motion detector flashing. I didn't care.

"Fuck me," I cried out and it became a race to see if we could orgasm before they got there. I already knew we would win because I was almost there.

"Eddie," I cried out as I crept over the hill to find release at the top. I screamed until my lungs ran out of air and the ripples running through me made me forget how to take a new breath. Eddie rode me down my own electric orgasm laying kisses all over me and nibbling on me until he found his own release.

Once we caught our breath Eddie slowly pulled out, sat me down. I pulled the condom off and threw it into a box of parts that would wind up in a junk yard.

"Kate," Eddie called my name, but I couldn't look at him as tears filled my eyes. I loved him. This act proved it and I didn't know how to handle it. "Fuck, Kate, are you okay? Do you want to talk about it?"

The police banged on the doors and shouted orders as my internal crazy train hit me head on with the realization that this was going to end so badly.

"I'm fine," I stated as I hurried into my clothes.

"Once we have a moment, we should talk about what just happened," he stated, but there was nothing to say.

"It was a mistake, my mistake," I whispered as the police banged on the doors again. "Listen to me, say nothing, do what they say, and Brooklyn will get you out."

We dressed and I grabbed my shoes on the way as I laid down and rolled under the human-doggy door to be greeted with guns.

"Climb out with your hands up," the officer screamed. At that moment I knew we were done for because he was a newbie.

"This is my father's garage. We are not trespassing," I stated as Eddie rolled out.

"Who is your father?" The second officer asked.

"Henry Huntington," I sighed knowing he was about to get a phone call. "Can you call Detective Mark Stone for me?" I asked and the cop started screaming again.

"Get on your belly and place your hands over your head with interlocking fingers."

I turned my head and saw Eddie and the look on his face was indecipherable. Whatever he was feeling he had encased behind a stone cold façade. I wanted to say something, but what was there to say.

"Miss Huntington do you have identification on you?" The second older officer asked and I pointed at my driver. My purse was still in the car.

"Who might you be?" He asked Eddie.

"Edward Wellington," he replied and the cop smiled.

"The medic?" The older cop asked and Eddie told him he was. Within minutes Eddie was off the ground and in handcuffs while he and the older officer talked about old times. While I laid on the ground waiting for my officers' testicles to drop.

"Miss Huntington, your father wishes to speak to you," the young cop said as he helped me up off the ground.

"Henry," I stated as I put the phone to my ear.

"You are going to go to jail. I imagine Brooklyn will be your next call and I won't stop it, but this might be that very moment when my parental actions help you turn your life around," Henry angrily spoke into the phone.

"But I don't do anything wrong anymore," I shouted. "All I do is work and go home. I'm a social leper, and you think jail can fix that?"

Nothing I said mattered, he felt he was doing the right thing and for Father's Day I was thinking he needed an auto-tightening neck tie with remote control, only I'd keep the controller. Just like that within minutes of hanging up we were arrested. As I watched Eddie get placed in the back of the older cop's car I knew I had lost the one man I had come to care for, and I had gotten part of my fantasy, which was amazing, except for the whole after its over part.

My mother should have named me tarnish because it was what I did to people and relationships. I watched as Eddie was driven away and wanted so badly to undo the last few hours.

How the hell could I love him? Did I know it was love? I had never been in love, so how could I possibly be sure.

Chapter 16

"When is our court date?" I asked Brooklyn as she had bailed out Eddie and me. "Can I take the fall so that Eddie doesn't get in trouble? I made him help me. Like gun point and everything," I lied and Brooklyn looked over at me and narrowed her eyes as if to study me. Then she pulled out of the parking lot and started home.

"Oh my God, you really like him," she blurted out with a laugh. "I never thought I would see the day Kate Huntington would like a guy so much she would take the rap for him."

"Brooklyn, it is not like that," I countered, but she could cut through my bullshit better than anyone else.

"Kate and Eddie sitting in a tree, f-u-c-k-i-n-g, first comes condoms and then comes vows, because he broke it and gave you a child," Brooklyn sang and I groaned.

"You are the worst friend," I whined and she laughed.

"Want me to return you to jail?"

"Thank you for getting us out," I replied with a sigh. Eddie had taken a cab home because Brooklyn wanted to talk to me. I hoped it wasn't about the case the entire police station was talking about. They said she was going to be the new Assistant District Attorney because she made the best bait for a serial killer.

I stopped thinking about it, and looked out the window as Brooklyn turned off the highway. Time flew by and I closed my eyes for only a little while and when I opened them we were sitting outside the Brooklyn bridge as a storm came in from the distance. The cluster in the sky made the sun beams shoot down on the bridge and it illuminated it. It was a religious sight to see.

"Do you know why I love this bridge so much?" Brooklyn asked and I shook my head. "It is strong and beautiful. People drive on her and stress her out every single day, but she stands tall, sturdy, and proud to take the abuse. This bridge reminds me of us. We both take the shit we are dealt and rise above it."

We sat in the car, and I knew Brooklyn well enough to know that when she went silent it is best not to say anything because whatever she had to say wouldn't be good.

"I have thought a lot about this, and I wanted to tell you first that I have accepted a job at the District Attorney's office, and am moving out."

"No," I said calmly as if it was my decision.

"Kate, Henry has already paid for the apartment and I found a beautiful place right near the office. They are making some adjustments I have requested and I move in a few weeks."

"Nope, it is not going to happen," I spoke in a soft whisper. Brooklyn was stubborn and I knew her mind was made up, but as her best friend I had to throw in my two cents. "The last Assistant District Attorney is all over the news because she turned up dead. I heard it on the radio just hours ago. Inside the police station it was the only thing they were talking about. I don't want that to be you."

"Kate, I love you, but I need to do this. I need to move forward in my life and you want to stay stagnant doing the same things over and over again. I want to get married, and have kids, but I can't do that if I am cleaning you up at 4AM after you puke up an insane amount of alcohol."

"Brooklyn I haven't had time to do that in months," I immediately got defensive.

"No, you have been working hard, and dealing with the -," she cut herself off before mentioning his name. "But if you were on a path to be a better adult I wouldn't have to bail you out of jail and get the charges dropped. You're welcome by the way," she stated sarcastically.

Brooklyn started the car back up and we traveled across the bright bridge before the storm blocked out the sun and it returned to the normal darkened state.

"Come to work with me tomorrow, see what happens to adults who don't mature."

Sitting in the courtroom is the most depressing place in the world as you watch people fight for their freedom. Brooklyn had mergered a deal between two companies needing buy-outs and now one was trying to back out after getting the payout.

I loved watching her in action it was like going to the symphony. You could see the music in her. Then a body sat down beside me and I looked over and smiled. Those cobalt blue eyes would make gorgeous babies one day for me to spoil.

"You come to watch the show?" I quietly asked Mark as he stared at Brooklyn.

"She is in her own world up there. She lights up the room when she argues her side," Mark softly replied.

"You come here and watch her often?" I asked and he nodded. "That is considered stalking detective," I tried to crack a joke, but the tone in my voice made it a fail.

"It has been a few weeks since I have seen you," I replied and he nodded his head. The bailiff looked over at me and told me to quiet down so Mark and I moved to the back of the courtroom.

"You get arrested and the first thing you do is ask the officer to call me, but not Brooklyn, she doesn't talk to me anymore," Mark sounded kind of upset, so I took it as an invite to pry.

"What did you expect?" I asked and those blue eyes held me hostage as he waited for an explanation. "She loved you every single day of her life. She waited for you to choose her, and yet you chose Mary. I shouldn't be talking to you either, but I kind of like you. Want to step outside for a minute."

Mark nodded and I stood up and walked out the door with him.

"What the hell are you talking about?" Mark asked and I nearly burst out laughing. *How could men be so blind?* "She never loved me. We went to Vegas to get married and run away, not because of love, but because we were kids and didn't know any better. I mean that would have been the time to tell me how she felt or any other day."

"You are preaching to the choir, but let me tell you it is not easy to tell people that. It's not easy to let them in your compound, past the guards, and then tell them they are in there and can do whatever they want when they have the weapons to destroy your fort."

"Your analogies are weird," Mark replied and I smiled. "The ship with Brooklyn sailed a long time ago, if she didn't tell me then that is not my fault."

"You should have seen it, Mark. She is still in love with you, but denies it to herself because you deny that you love her too." I spoke softly as people filed in around us. I almost felt horrid for Brooklyn. To know that the man she loved the most didn't have a clue how she felt.

Then everything in my existence halted as a chain clinking limp sounded down the hallway and the hair on my neck stood up. I turned my head and stared at Kurt wearing a white and black jumpsuit in shackles limping down the hall. He smiled at me and I grabbed Mark and pulled him to me.

"You're okay," Mark whispered, but I wasn't my entire body was shaking, my mind was racing, and my heart was doing laps on its own race track. "He is never going to hurt you again," Mark reassured me as he wrapped his arms around me. I fought to get loose, and yet I fought to stay in his arms. I didn't know what I wanted and it brought tears to my eyes.

"What is he doing here?" I asked as I gripped Mark's shirt in my fists and kept my head down as the chills and horrid taste in my mouth overwhelmed me.

"His lawyer is asking for a bail reduction so he can be able to make some game before the trial."

"Will they let him do that?" I asked and Mark didn't answer. I knew he didn't know the answer, but I needed him to say no.

"He is in shackles, and is not going to get through me to harm you. When you are not with me remember that even if they set him loose you have a restraining order. He can't come near you."

"What is that piece of paper going to fix?" I asked vehemently. "Nothing! There are laws about hitting people, but he did that just fine even with that in place. If he gets out that restraining order won't keep him away."

"I can request a detail for you, and you can call 911 if he comes near you again, but let's not get ahead of ourselves. He hasn't made bail," Mark spoke like a detective and not a friend as he brought my worst fears down to just a hint of panic. It was a little weird that he was rubbing my shoulders, but I understood why. He saw me as his little sister and didn't want me to worry.

"I love you, you big dumb ox," I murmured against him as I hugged Mark tight.

"You better?" He asked and I nodded as I wiped the last stray tear from my face. "Good! Now get in there and take care of my girl," Mark stated as he turned me around and gave me a pat on the butt. I knew he was about to follow Kurt, and make sure he stayed away. It was almost liberating being with Mark because for a moment I felt like the old Kate. I flung my hair and looked over my shoulder to get the last word.

"She's my girl because you didn't put a ring on it," I kept a straight face till I was through and then smiled as I walked back in the courtroom where everyone was packing up.

"Where have you been?" Brooklyn asked as I walked up to her table.

"Talking to Mark," I stated nonchalantly.

"He was here?" Brooklyn asked as she fixed her black skirt and her cobalt eyes scoured the room looking for him. She fixed her lilac silk shirt and did a unnoticed hair flip to look behind her. This girl had it bad.

"Yes, he was in here watching you, but I wanted to talk to him so we went in the hallway."

"You okay?" Brooklyn asked with concern.

"Yea, I'll be fine. I just needed Mark to stop eye fucking you beside me," I sarcastically retorted.

"What is it you are not telling me?" Brooklyn asked as she waded through my bullshit. "What is going on?" I didn't want to tell her I had seen Kurt. I wasn't sure why I felt so anxious about talking about it so I tried in a narrative manner.

"This guy I dated-," Brooklyn cut me off.

"Some guy you fucked. Dating implies doing something together with your legs shut," she corrected me.

"Fine, this guy I fucked on a Zamboni was out there and it freaked me out a little, so Mark calmed me down."

"You saw Kurt?"

"How the hell did you get him from that?" I asked.

"Zamboni," Brooklyn replied. "I forgot-," she started and got cut off by a messenger handing her files. "I forgot he had asked for the hearing."

"You knew?" I asked with shock.

"Kate, listen to me," Brooklyn spoke and I really tried to hear her, but it was all jumbled.

"Just stop," I said as my limit for daily what the fucks had reached its fill. "I know you didn't expect me to be here, but when was anyone going to tell me?"

"We weren't going to unless he makes bail," Brooklyn sighed. "The Assistant District Attorney Gloria Peterson is handling it and there shouldn't be an issue."

"Where the fuck is Taylor?" I bellowed and everyone left in the court room looked my way.

"Taylor is at a meeting with the Mayor and Commissioner. Gloria steps in in his absence. She is really good. I wouldn't worry unless you have too."

"You sure she is good?" I asked and Brooklyn nodded. "If you and her were up against each other who would win?"

"Depending on the facts, evidence, and other things," Brooklyn started, but then hesitated as she looked over at me. Then a smile spread across her face. "I would win. Didn't anyone tell you I'm bad ass?"

I laughed and so did she as she leaned over and gave me a hug.

"That asshole can't even pee without crying, so do not worry about him," she whispered into my ear.

"You ready to go?" She asked and I nodded.

We headed home to change clothes. I put on a pair of jeggings and an extra-long maroon sweater with my black Uggs. Brooklyn broke into my closet for once and took a navy blue ribbed sweater a pair of skinny jeans and my other Uggs.

Then we grabbed take out and headed to my mom's house to see how she was doing. When we pulled up outside her house we saw Henry's Porsche in the driveway. Seeing his car just pissed me off. Wherever he went frustration followed. I wondered what he was doing there, and was going to find out. Then I opened the door before the driver had it in park and got out of the car and walked right inside the little ranch style house.

The newly painted burgundy walls looked like someone tried to cover up a murder and it made me take a step back. There was new carpet, it was such a light beige it was almost white. What the hell had happened to the pale yellow walls and navy blue carpet that we once had.

"Who the hell vomited Dr. Pepper on your walls?" I asked my mom who was laying in her recliner with a blanket.

"I did," Liza spoke up as she walked out of the hallway with a man holding a notebook as she pointed out things to change. She was dressed in a black silk dress as if she were ready for the Met Gala. This woman had no class.

"Hey, boob-a-trocious. What the hell are you doing to my house?" I asked as she scoffed. I turned on Henry who was in jeans and a t-shirt looking like a homeless man. "What the hell is tyrannosaurus twit doing?"

"Kate, be nice," my mom called out in a gravelly voice. Brooklyn took that moment to walk in the door with the food. "They are taking care of me."

"Looks like they are helping themselves to everything you have worked for," I gritted through my teeth as anger enraged me.

"We made a deal," Liza spoke up and I wanted to thump her like the annoying little gnat she was. "We are taking care of your moms medical bills in exchange we get the house when she croaks."

I lunged for her and found Brooklyn and Henry holding me from killing her.

"You fucking bitch," I screamed and Liza calmly walked over to me knowing that Brooklyn and Henry wouldn't let me go. She tapped my nose with a pencil and whispered. "Tell me did you enjoy your time in jail? Must be nice to be with other dykes. Play nice and I might let you get your things from here when your mom is six feet under."

That was all it took for everything in my world to focus on the bullseye she just put on herself. I started dragging Brooklyn across the floor as I elbowed Henry in the nose. Blood poured onto the almost white carpet and Liza shrieked. The nurse came out of a back room to see what the commotion was. She inserted herself between me and the blond bimbo who needed to die.

"Stop!" She shouted. "This isn't healthy for my patient and I am going to have to ask you all to leave."

The nurse wouldn't step away from the front of me, and Brooklyn wouldn't let go as Henry left out the front door with blood pouring out of his nose and down his shirt. Liza took her assistant and pushed him out the door when she turned and looked at me.

"Can't hit me I'm pregnant," she called out with a wink.

"No, I can hit everything except your stomach," I retorted and she scurried to the car.

"Kate," my mom called and my focus readjusted. "Why do you insist on fighting with them?"

"Mom, it has always been you and I. With Mike starting over with a new job I want to take care of you and the bills. I can do this mom. I want to take care of you the way you always took care of me."

She waved me over and I went and sat on the couch right beside her recliner. The nurse voiced her displeasure, but I didn't care. I held onto my mom's hand.

"Sometimes even soda pop girls need a little help," my mom whispered and I cringed. "My coke is going flat. The doctor called tonight and said that my levels just are dwindling and if it continues chemo won't be an option any longer."

I didn't acknowledge her. I looked down as the world I once knew was now a strange foreign land. There were several people in my life that I would die for and my mom topped that list. It killed me to know that there was nothing I could do to stop what was happening to her.

"How much time?" I asked and my mom and Brooklyn shared a look. Then Brooklyn came over and sat beside me. I knew it was bad at that moment. "Damn it mom, how long do I have with you?"

"A few weeks at most if we stop treatment now. If we continue it will be days."

I couldn't breathe. My vision tunneled and everything turned gray around the lamp I was focused in on. A few days to weeks. That wasn't enough time to make her proud of me. It just wasn't enough time for me to be able to tell her goodbye.

"Kate," she whispered bringing my focus back to her. "I already told Mike when he came by. He went to the bank, and came back with a check, giving me every dime he had and even gave me the deed to his house. Henry is taking it along with this one to cover my bills. The last thing I want is to leave a burden on any of you."

Mike had given her everything he had.

Brooklyn was leaving.

My mom was dying.

Kurt might go free, and...

The one person I wanted to share this with was arrested because of me. What else could the world take from me before I hit bottom. I had thought I was already there, but I learned in the last few minutes that I wasn't at bottom. This was it, and the feeling sucked.

Chapter 17

The next day came and I was terrified out of my mind to walk into the building. I closed my eyes as I stared up the skyscraper. *I can be Kate, I can be Kate, I got this because I am Kate.* I chanted it over and over again as I tried to find courage.

"Hello," I asked as my phone rang without even checking to see who it was.

"How is the cherry to my coke?" My mom asked and I smiled.

"You always seem to know when I need you," I replied and I could almost envision her interest getting piqued.

"What is going on?" She asked and I explained where I was and what was going on. "Kate, listen to me. I know the two of you don't like each other very much, but that is my fault. Had he been allowed to know about you things would be different."

"Why did you hide me?" I asked the one question I never dared to ask before. I didn't want to know, but I did.

"I was like you, Kate. I didn't spend more than a night or two with a man. It was a very lonely life, and when Henry came along he was fun, always going places. He was different, he gave me a reason to stay."

"Did you love him?" I asked and held my breath while I waited for the answer.

"No, I never got a chance to fall in love with him, because a month into my relationship with Henry I met Mike. I loved him the second I saw him. I just always wanted to be near him, and tell him everything. I wanted to make him dinner and tell him every joke I had ever heard. He was the one, but we ended it. Even if I would have gone back he didn't take me being pregnant with someone else's baby while we were dating as a good thing.

"Mike loved me so much that even though we broke up he stayed. For the next twenty-seven years we lived in a partnership of love."

"Why did you have to tell him you had his child? I mean mom he is the Anti-Christ."

"I was getting sick a lot more frequent and wanted you to know where you came from. More importantly I wanted you to stop living your life the way you were before something bad happened-," my mom sighed into the phone, and I knew she had more to say, but she was thinking about Kurt and was starting to cry.

"I'm fine, mom." I replied. "Don't cry for me."

"You are not okay, Kate. You found your Mike in Eddie. Everyone around us can see it. When you are with him you aren't angry or bitter. You have fun, laugh, smile, and you are whole."

"Mom, he is not going to be your son in law," I quickly retorted.

"Just take the day and think about where you would be right now without him. Don't tell me now. Tell me when you come to dinner tonight."

I agreed and hung up the phone as exhaustion plagued her. Then I walked inside. I took a deep breath as I walked into the security office and everyone stood up and greeted me with apologies. It merely made me mad. Where were they when I needed them?

"Where do I need to go to start today?" I asked and they all looked at each other.

"Mr. Huntington didn't put you on the list. He said you couldn't work for him so he was going to stick you with someone else, but never told us who."

That just pissed me the hell off. I dragged my ass out of bed at 5AM to take a shower, and be here by 6:30AM so I could start his work day, and he didn't even know what closet of an office he was shoving me into. I snatched up securities phone and dialed his extension.

"Mr. Huntington's office," one of the blond minions answered.

"Tell him his spawn of Satan is on her way up."

I walked away from everyone at that point and took the elevator up to the seventy second floor. As the doors parted I heard the protesting that I had hung up on and walked right past them. I flung open the office doors.

"Hello dad," I shouted over the staff members seated in his office. "I thought I would come tell you myself that I was quitting my birth right given job here and taking up prostitution. There is good money in it. I love the drugs, cock, and my pimp treats me good."

Henry had the room cleared in under five seconds it was a sight to see. I internally smirked that my mouth had won some imaginary clear the room award.

"Kathryn, what the hell is your problem? Were you raised by wolves? Did your mother forget to teach you manners?"

I squinted my eyes and snarled as the rage I felt coursed through me heating my veins as I stared at the bullseye on his face. I wanted to punch him.

"My fucking name is Kate! Get it right and while you are doing that get me a position because I didn't come all the way down here for nothing!"

His assistant came in the door and I turned to look at her. "What the hell do you want Cara?" I asked and she started closing the double doors.

"Her name is Carly," Henry corrected me.

"Oh sure you know her fucking name," I yelled sarcastically.

"How do you even know her?" Henry asked and I smirked.

"I ate her pussy in the office of your garage," I lied as we stood there across from each other. Neither of us seemed to want to back down.

"Well then at least you have one friend here. I had someone volunteer to take you on. They were warned about your attitude, attire, and asinine judgment.

"There are rules. The first one is a given, do not get fired. If you do get fired you will be moved to another part of the office, something with longer hours and less pay. Do not have sex in the office, or with any of my staff. Dress like you want to keep your job and not like you just stepped off the street corner. You will show respect when talking to me or about me in this office as well. Lastly, when Liza is in this building you will refrain from calling her anything derogatory which includes 'slurpy slut' which is what you addressed her Easter card with."

"One last thing, no more flowers from your sexual partners it is ridiculous."

I crossed my arms while I stewed over everything he said. All I had to do was file papers, and be nice to him and his wife. *This was going to be harder than I thought.*

"You will be working on the thirty ninth floor under-," I cut him off.

"What partners are you talking about?" I asked because I was pretty sure the men I met didn't fall into the Monday through Friday, Seven to Seven type jobs.

Henry wiggled his finger and opened a door to an empty office that across from him. Inside sat almost a hundred bouquets.

"What is this?" I demanded to know.

"They have been coming every half hour or so since yesterday. It has to stop."

I walked in and picked up one of the cards that a teddy bear was holding.

Please call me.

I miss you.

I love you.

Kurt.

"What the fuck?" I shouted as my body fluctuated between fear and rage. I grabbed my cell phone. I made all the appropriate calls hiding the quiver in my voice as they one by one told what I already knew. I went into the conference room and waited as Mark was coming to get the evidence.

"He was released on bail," Mark told me as I sat in a conference room a few hours later. "The judge felt that a five-million-dollar bond was high so she dropped it to two million and he put his house up."

"So he is out there?" I asked as I crossed my arms over my body. I turned to look at Taylor who had sat at the table and said nothing.

"I'm so sorry Kate," Taylor finally spoke in a manner that had me looking at him crossly. He couldn't even look me in the eye.

"What is it you are not saying?" I demanded. Then I looked over at Mark. "What?"

"They threw out the security video of the attack because it was not obtained with a warrant. The original detective said someone delivered it to his doorstep and he never obtained the warrant to collect the actual one instead of the copy."

"You can get a warrant and go get the original then, right?" I asked as I grabbed a chair and sat down.

"I'm sorry Kate, the video overlaps every five days and by the time we found out it was gone."

Mark walked over and put his hands on my shoulders as he leaned down and kissed my head.

"Someone had to be with you, Kate. There is no way you moved his unconscious body with a fractured collar bone. If we knew who was there they could attest to what happened," Taylor spoke as his hands made fists. I knew he was getting aggravated with me, but I couldn't remember.

"I don't remember, anything," I stated with my own frustration.

"Kate," Mark spoke quietly. "I want to put a detail on you for a little while."

"Why?"

"Just a precaution," Mark stated as he pulled out the chair beside me and took my hand.

"You gonna marry Brooklyn?" I asked changing the subject and Mark took the bait.

"Think she will have me still? You can wear a fluorescent orange gown to match those traffic cones Eddie was talking about."

I rolled my eyes and then my attention turned to the door. Taylors assistant walked in and handed him a note. He read it, signed it, and passed it back. *Did she follow him like a shadow or more like a dog and heeled when told?*

"Kate," Taylor asked with restraint, he looked like he wanted to punch someone, but his voice was cool and mellow. "Can you tell me how many sexual partners you have had?"

"That is none of your business." I declared.

"It is now. Kurt's lawyer is stating that he can bring in your sexual partners to say that you had sex with them in exchange for alcohol."

"Maybe, the alcohol made me drunk and I made bad choices," I replied sarcastically.

"Kate they want you charged with prostitution. That you exchanged sexual favors for things of monetary value."

"Are you fucking kidding me?" I asked as I stood up and my chair went flying. "I'm a hooker because I didn't want him to put anything of his on me, or in me. *Me?* I'm a damn prostitute because I didn't want him to hit me over and over again? Do I look like a camera-less porn star?

I marched out of the office with fury racing through me. I wanted to get fired. I wanted to go down in a blaze of glory. I wanted to break every rule. I looked at my hand as I got in the elevator and pressed the thirty ninth floor.

I fucked people for no reason. Some bought me drinks, some didn't. Just like some were good in bed and others became the reason I got pickier.

I exited the elevator, walked down a hall, and flung the last office door on the corner open. I took my purse off over my shoulder with my back to whoever my new boss was. I tried to calm my rage, but I wanted to steal back my life and say fuck the world all at the same time.

"I need you to bend me over your desk, spank me, fuck me, and smile for the camera," I stated quickly. I had to shake off the flowers, the possible charges, and piss off Henry in that order. There was no better way than to fuck for free. Plus, my need for a fix was high.

The glass walls had a white film on them to keep people from seeing inside the office, but I knew security had cameras in everywhere. I turned to look at the choking noise to see Eddie coughing out his coffee.

"What the fuck are you doing here?"

Chapter 18

"Excuse me?" Eddie asked as his coughing slowed and he walked into his office bathroom and started soaking up the liquid off his pants.

"You're my boss?" I asked in disbelief. I heard the white noise from an intercom and changed my attitude.

"Edward Wellington, Chief Financial Officer, and your new boss. Now as your boss I am going to pretend I heard you incorrectly and give you a chance to say something different."

"What do you think I said?" I asked playing coy. I ran my fingers across his oak desk seductively as I moved down the front of it. I shifted some papers and climbed onto his desk. "All you have to do is sit in this chair and you will have the best lunch of your life."

I heard a buzz as I placed my legs on either side of his empty chair spreading the tight skirt of my dress as much as I could. I heard it once more and then my sperm donor echoed through the room.

"Get off his desk!" Henry bellowed. "It would help you along Kate if you remember I am always one step ahead. That little stunt might have worked elsewhere to get you fired, but Mr. Wellington is gay!"

"What?" Eddie and I shouted at the same time. We both looked at each other and I busted out laughing. I climbed off the desk and looked around to see where he could see me.

"Henry, send the flowers to every woman who works here and give me five minutes with my new boss. I need to know just how gay he really is."

"Kate," the voice came through the speaker as I whispered to Eddie. "Is there a way to turn off your intercom so no one hears me?"

"Yea, I will unplug it for a few minutes."

"Is that all it takes to get you off?" I asked out of defiance as I pulled a blue post it note and wrote the words 'suck it' on the back and hung it over the camera in the corner of the room. When I turned back Eddie was unplugging a cord coming out of his desk.

"I was warned that my new employee could be trouble, but I never once thought you would start your work day like this," Eddie admitted as he sat back down in his chair.

"I'm sorry," I whispered as I swallowed my pride to admit to my mistake. It was no longer funny. "I wasn't – I mean, what are you. So you're bi? What I mean is – Ugh, I didn't mean to offend-," Eddie held up his hand and cut me off.

"I am offended that everyone thinks I am gay or bi-sexual," he stated and I busted out laughing again.

"I'm sorry," I said through the laughter. "When I decide to make impressions I go all out. What are you really doing here?"

"I am Henry's CFO (chief financial officer). I work directly for him, and now you are my new assistant."

"Is this a joke?" I asked as I walked over and looked out the wall of windows at the great big city I loved so much.

"Not a joke. They were going to stick you in some job you would have hated, with barely any pay, and longer hours than I work in a week."

"You are my boss?" I asked as the phrase sank in. So far today I had been a soda pop girl from a one-night stand. An ungrateful daughter. A prostitute who fucks for beer, and now I was the employee of the only man I could see as fuckable. I apparently was the jack of all trades and it wasn't even 9AM.

"I am your boss," Eddie replied. "I ask that you don't cuss, maintain professional behavior, and don't call me Eddie here."

I suddenly felt ashamed of myself for the first time. I was going to work under this man and had already cussed at him, hit on him, slept beside him, fucked him, and had given him a full dose of myself.

"Do you want to start over? From the moment we met and go from there?" I asked quietly.

"My first impression of you was you calling me an asshat and telling me I didn't know how to treat a lady. Is that what you want to go back to?"

"My first impression was of you ratting me out," I replied defensively.

"How about we call that a truce and we forget the spanking and get to work, or shall I pull up your skirt nice and slow while you bend over and spank you for every infraction you have committed since I met you?" Eddie asked and I swallowed hard.

That sounded enticing when it shouldn't. I felt like it was a trap, and I wasn't walking into it. I nodded my head and went to shake his hand.

"Truce."

"You really are Henry Huntington's daughter?" Eddie asked as he was going over the daily tasks I would be assigned to do.

"That is what they tell me," I replied.

"How is your mom?" Eddie asked and I could feel my body lighting up as I told him about every single miniscule bit of progress she made, but then I had to tell him the bitterness of her health.

"I'm so sorry," he replied and I nodded. "If there is anything you need let me know."

"I need to know why you haven't called since we got arrested."

"Kate, you didn't know me and I pushed my way into your life. I knew you were vulnerable and could be there when you needed someone and it would give me a permanent home in your world, but that is not what I wanted."

"What did you want?" I asked softly as stood in front of his desk.

"You. I wanted to know everything about you inside and out. I wanted to take your pain and make it mine so you didn't have to feel it. I wanted to kiss you until I was all you knew."

"What stopped you?" I asked as nausea rose up in my belly. He was talking about commitments, and long term things and that stuff made me freak out.

"You," Eddie replied. "Even through your mild anxiety you gave yourself freely to me. It was like you had finally found what you needed, but the way I entered your life felt like a manipulation. Your actions after we fucked made it seem like maybe I had pushed you too far when you were vulnerable and I was taking advantage of you."

"We don't know each other completely so I will let it slide, but if I want you gone you will be gone, but until I say those words, don't leave me assuming that it is what is best for me," I placed my hands on my hips suddenly extremely upset that he was willing to stay away. I wanted him to chase me, even when I didn't want him too. I was a contradictory person.

This was not the way I intended to start a new job, but as I put my things away I had to laugh. If anyone could ever leave a hellacious first impression, it would be me.

"Let's go over this one more time," Eddie proceeded to repeat himself for the thousandth time.

"I got it when you don't want to take a call I get the name and number, what it is regarding, and then I tell them that you are out of your office for the day, even though you never go anywhere," I replied and Eddie smiled.

"I think you got it now," he laughed and went back into his office.

The days had flown by and every day at lunch I would sit at my desk, call my mom, and check on her. Then when five rolled around I would grab dinner so that Eddie and I could eat with my mom and Mike.

"Mr. Wellington's office this is Kate how can I help you?"

"This is Daisy, put me through," a woman demanded on the other line. I followed protocol and took her name and number and then when she got aggravated and started yelling I merely placed her on hold and knocked on his office door.

"Come in," he called out and I pushed the door open and then closed it leaning up against it. I had a pink slip of paper with her information on it, but when I looked at him I didn't want to give it to him.

I got a jealous twinge. I knew he wasn't married because he didn't wear a ring, but maybe he had a girlfriend. I instantly wanted to punch something at the thought of him with someone else, and yet I didn't want to want him. "Miss Huntington," Eddie said in question when I turned the lock behind my back.

"I don't know how to do this," I admitted and my cheeks flamed with embarrassment. "I haven't been with the same person more than once in a long time. I only see guys once."

Eddie tilted his head, leaned back in his chair, and took a sip from his coffee. I hated when he didn't speak because it always made me feel like I had to say more.

"I – um – have an itch, that needs to be scratched," I tried to explain and he sat back and smiled.

"You should see a doctor about that," he replied and I laughed.

"Do you want to play doctor?" I asked and I saw the glimmer in his eyes.

"I'm not a doctor, Miss Huntington, I am your boss. Always the boss."

"Well then Mr. Wellington," I started walking toward him. "I have a message for you," I seductively whispered. Then I walked over to his desk and bent over it with the note in my hand.

"What is the message?" He asked as he stood up and walked around his desk.

"I forgot," I whispered as I dropped her message on the desk.

This was easier than I thought. I was so uptight, but a couple laughs with him and I was comfortable with whatever he wanted to do. Well most anything. To this day I couldn't put a straw in my mouth without wanting to vomit.

"I think you should be punished, Miss Huntington," Eddie played along. He bent over the top of me and I could feel his hardened cock in the between my legs. "You sure you are okay with this?" He whispered and I nodded. "Close your eyes. Relax and take a deep breath. You are safe with me. I'm going to spank you," he spoke softly and I felt the breath in my ear and then his lips on my shoulder. "Are you okay with that?" He asked. I know he was worried because of what Kurt had done, but I didn't fear Eddie.

"I'm okay," I whispered as he grabbed my hair and jerked it back. Just like that I was lost in the euphoria of Eddie and broke my own rules about sleeping with men twice.

After we finished, we cleaned up and went to lunch. He took me to this tiny little vendor and I had to laugh. Most guys wanted to take me to five star restaurants, but not Eddie. He took me to a diner on wheels.

"It's taco Tuesday," he stated as if to explain why I wasn't sitting in some restaurant where the staircase was laced in gold. I laughed at the genuine way he was with me. There was no rush to get me into bed. There was no pressure to be someone else. There was no reason to lie. Being with him was just easy.

We took our plates and went and sat at a picnic table near the edge of Bryant Park and watched as kids played soccer and moms did group exercise. We sat across from each other and that twinkle in Eddie's eye told me he liked me. It caused my stomach to drop so before he could bring it up I shoved food in my mouth.

"I love taco Tuesday," I replied as I shoved a chicken taco into my mouth and lettuce fell onto my plate.

"You are perfect, Kate Huntington, don't let anyone ever tell you that you are not."

"I bet you say that to all the ladies that come into your office and want to fuck you," I joked.

"Kate, I am being serious. I thought the first time was because you were fighting so hard to get yourself back, but it's you. When you give yourself, you do it fully with no reservation, no body image issues, no fear of lights being on or off, you have no restrictions, and you trust, fully. You are the girl every man dreams to find."

I was suddenly very uncomfortable with the words he chose. Every man just wanted to get laid, they were not out looking for me, they were looking for a pussy to dive into.

"This stuff scares the hell out of me Eddie and I usually run," I looked away with my admission, trying to hide from his judgment, but there never was any with him. He always accepted who I was and what I could give and never really asked for more.

"If you run, I will chase you," he replied. "Kate, whether you believe it or not you are worth the chase where others are not."

"This was just an itch that got scratched," I clarified just so we both knew where it stood.

"Well nurse, I think I might have another itch tomorrow during lunch," Eddie quickly retorted and I smiled.

"Wings Wednesday?" I asked and Eddie nodded with a chuckle. "It's a non-date date."

Chapter 19

I was living in my little euphoric bubble. Every day I looked forward to my morning coffee with Brooklyn, making sure I was Eddie's daily lunch, and having dinner with my mom and Mike. I occasionally had to go to lunch with Henry as it got closer to the babies' due date.

I dressed in a tight black dress that had a large white calla lily on the hip. I curled my hair and added a white calla lily clip to hold my hair back from my face. I was actually started to love my job, every time I got angry Eddie and I laughed about it, and more importantly I wasn't freaking out about fucking Eddie more than once.

"Hey Brook," I answered my phone as I grabbed my keys and headed down the elevator.

"Kate, how much do you love me?" Brooklyn asked and I took a pause.

"What have you done?" I immediately questioned her.

"I got us a two-day spa package in the Hamptons. Talk to your boss-cock and see if you can get off this weekend," she snickered.

"Sounds like fun. I will talk to him," I continued talking to her about nothing important until I pulled up outside the office. "Got to go, I'm already late."

Then I hung up and went upstairs. There was some big meeting this morning so no one noticed I was running a few minutes late. I sat down at my desk to see a single red rose sitting on my keyboard and smiled. Before I could even spare a full thought the phone rang.

"Mr. Wellington's office this is Kate how can I help you?" I asked as I put the head set on and unraveled the cords.

"Hi, Kate," a familiar voice sounded on the line.

"Who is this?" I asked and grabbed my memo pad and a pen.

"Kurt," he replied and my stomach sank. I hung up and the phone rang again.

"Mr. Wellington's office this is Kate how can I help you?"

"I miss you Kate," Kurt said in a demonic tone. "Seems you and I have a date with destiny. You jump, I jump, isn't that how your boyfriend put it."

I hung up again. Then the phone rang again.

"Mr. Wellington's office this is Kate how can I help you?"

"I just wanted to ask you a question," Kurt growled.

"If you will go away and stop calling I will answer."

"What would you do if tomorrow Edward took a tumble down thirty-nine flights of stairs and died. Would you surrender -,"

"Kurt," I cut him off. "I have to go my boss is looking at me." I lied, but I had to get him off the phone. As I kicked my heels off ready to run and the cord wrapped around my feet.

"No he isn't, Kate, and you are an awful liar."

"Yes, I swear to you he is," I lied again, and was contemplating hanging up on him again.

"Don't lie to me," Kurt screamed into the phone. I heard him take some deep breaths and then with a lowered quiet voice he said the words that made me jump. "I can see you Kate, and the next time you lie to me it will be your blood dripping down your body."

I stood up as the feeling of being stalked plagued me. I did a 360-degree spin on the room as chills traveled down my spine and nerves fluttered through me. I saw a shadow in the open elevator, but didn't see anyone. The phone cord caught around me and ripped my headset off when Kurt started to laugh.

I fought with the cord in a panic to untangle myself as Eddie walked by.

"Kate, you okay?" Eddie questioned me before he saw I had wrapped myself. "Are you and the phone fighting?" He asked with a smile. I nodded as I fought the tremors that wracked my body. I searched the room again as Eddie walked into his office. By the time, I got the cord off me, plugged it back in, and sat back down. Eddie was right there again. I took a deep breath and forced myself to hide in, bury it deep inside me where it could never resurface.

"Kate," Eddie called out behind me. "Are you okay? You are really pale?" He asked as he placed his palm on my forehead. "Are you sick?" He asked and I shook my head. "Okay well I am going downstairs, hold my calls okay?"

"No," I shouted too loudly. "You need to stay here I lost connection with an important call and they might call back. Will you wait till tomorrow to drop off those forms?"

"Sure," Eddie nodded. "I have some other work to do, let me know if whoever it was calls back."

When the phone rang again I stared at the light that flickered to tell me what line. I stared because I didn't know if it would be him again or not.

"Mr. Wellington's office, this is Kate, how can I help you?" I finally answered on the fourth ring, right before voicemail picked up.

"Mr. Wellington, please," a feminine voice came across the line.

"Can I get your name please?"

"He will know my name, just put me through," the women sounded annoyed.

"Policy states that I get your name and number prior to transferring," I replied trying to sound completely business like.

"Daisy," she replied and I wrote down her name and number. "Now transfer the damn line, or should I wait on hold and listen to you fuck him again?"

The real me wanted to reach through the phone and pluck out every hair she had on her head, but I needed this job, and Eddie needed to be able to keep his.

"I'm sorry ma'am we have had trouble with our lines, but I can assure you I am not sleeping with him," I lied. If Henry found out we were fucking we would both be jobless, but if I pissed off a potential client, like she might be, I would be homeless and working in the mailroom for peanuts per hour.

I transferred her to his voicemail anyway – oops – and then I cleared the line. Within seconds it rang again and both Kurt and her made me not want to answer any more calls.

I answered on the second ring this time, prepared to apologize.

"Mr. Wellington's office, this is Kate, how can I help you?"

"Miss Huntington, you have the sexiest phone voice ever," Brooklyn teased.

"You are going to get me into trouble," I whispered and Brooklyn laughed.

"Since when do you care about getting into trouble? I became a lawyer just so I could defend you."

"I got the impression, okay I heard a rumor, that if Eddie can't handle me then I will be transferred, but he will be fired. Henry knows that kind of pressure will keep me in line. I don't want Eddie to lose his job like Mike did."

"Kate Huntington, you do like him. It is like a dream come true. I can see wedding bells and baby strollers. You seriously like this guy," Brooklyn stated with fake shock.

"I just don't want to see him lose his job like Mike lost his," I whispered into the phone.

"Honey, that man will not lose his job over you. He might lose his manhood, pride, ego, or he might lose his load, but his job will still be there. Stop listening to water cooler talk, half of it is bullshit anyway."

"Easier said than done," I replied as I looked over my right shoulder to see if I could see Eddie.

"I was just calling to let you know that I was giving you the night off."

"What?" I asked with slight hesitation.

"In about ten minutes Eddie will receive a package couriered from my office. Inside will be an itinerary. You will get one emailed to you as well."

"Brooklyn, what the hell is this?" I nearly shouted and had to remember I was at work. I looked over at the elevator as it dinged and there was a short man with curly red hair with a envelope heading right for Eddie's office.

"Kate, listen to me. I know you put up a wall with fucking him because you are scared of letting him in. You are terrified of allowing him to care for you, but this isn't the way to live. You will be under NYPD protection the whole night so nothing you don't want to happen will, and whatever does happen we can talk out over the weekend while we get waxed, plucked, and massaged."

"Why are you doing this?" I asked in a panic as Eddie signed for the envelope.

"I know Kurt got out of prison, and while you have been trying to keep up appearances I see right thru you. You are letting that asshole deter you from finding your own happiness. That dickless fucker will not be the reason that you shied away from Eddie when he needs you to take the next step."

"Brook," I said with a childish whimper. I didn't know how to act or what to say so I whimpered like a scolded dog, but for no real reason.

"What is done is done. Besides I love a love story with a happy ending. Now go get it for the both of us."

"Brook, I don't like this. I would rather be at home," I rushed out my words.

"I know, but your mom wants a son in law. Her words not mine."

"Of course she does," I replied as the elevator chimed again. Another courier came out and walked right up to my desk.

"Sign here," he stated and I did as he handed me a gift wrapped present.

"What did you get me?" I asked Brooklyn as a smile crossed my face. I loved gifts.

"Kate, I didn't send you anything," she stated shortly as conversations around her picked up.

"Brooklyn, you got spa tickets, and are sending Eddie and I out, and then I got this box. Who else would send me something?" I tore open the purple package and lifted the lid.

"AHH," I screamed into the phone.

"What is it?" Brooklyn screamed in the headset. "Kate, talk to me," Brooklyn shouted. "Kate," she screamed again as Eddie came flying out of his office. I couldn't breathe. I fell to the floor and tried to scoot away but the headset was tangled around me. "Get me Taylor Cross and Mark Stone on conference, now!" Brooklyn bellowed in my ear.

"Lisa, call the police, get me Detective Stone, and put him on my private line," Eddie shouted as I kicked and wiggled to get loose. Everyone was watching as I sobbed on the floor. Eddie was on his wireless headset as he held me.

"Mark, you better get over here now," I heard Eddie say. "Someone just killed Liza Huntington and sent the head to Kate."

Chapter 20

"It was him wasn't it?" I asked as the medics covered me in a gray blanket. Eddie had yet to leave my side. Henry had come down to identify his wife and then left when he found out that the baby had been cut out of her and taken to the hospital. It was a healthy four-pound baby girl.

"Kate," Mark sighed and he sat on the floor so he could look me in the eye. "I have to ask you this. Did you recently threaten to kill, try to injure, or harm the victim?"

"Mark, you know me. Of course I did. I threaten the mail man if he drops a package."

"Then Kate I have to tell you not to leave town, and a different detective will handle this as it is a conflict of interest for me to question you further."

I nodded as Mark leaned forward and placed a kiss on my cheek. Then he made a few phone calls and left.

"Where is she?" Brooklyn yelled at everyone the second she got off the elevator. I raised my hand like we were in elementary school and she bolted for the floor. Eddie let go so Brook could wrap me in her arms. "I'm so sorry, I'm so sorry. I will fucking murder him for this," she whispered as I held onto her.

"You are not to talk to the police without me present. You are on a protection detail until further notice."

"Why?" I asked as Brooklyn pulled back and I numbly stared at her. I had gone past the fear, and panic. I had left anxiety in the dust, and now there was nothing there. Any emotion was too harsh, so there were none left in me. "We don't even know it was him."

Brook sat back on her heels and looked strangely at me. Then she looked up at Eddie and he shook his head nonchalantly like I wasn't supposed to see.

"Oh, what now?" I exclaimed with irritation. "I am so tired of all the damn secrets from here on out. I am the only one with a secret."

Then I felt tired. Using any feeling as all were exhausting and I didn't really want to do it anymore. Brooklyn took my hand in hers and stared at me. When she got quiet you knew it was bad.

"Honey," Brooklyn spoke excessively quiet. "There was a note."

She pulled up her phone to show me a note that the corners had been saturated in blood, but you could still read the majority of it.

Roses are red

Violets are pale

Guess who you should've killed

Cause now I'm out of jail.

Took care of this problem for you, so now we can be together without any negativity in your life.

Love even into death

Kurt

I stared at the phone while Brooklyn and Eddie talked to the cops around me. I was in a state of shock. I hated Liza and wanted her dead twenty-three hours of the day, but I never anticipated anyone killing her.

"Come on," Eddie spoke softly as he lifted me up on my feet. "We have to go," he said, but I was in some other place. I didn't know where we were going, but I knew we were moving down in the elevator.

We climbed into the back of a police SUV and rode away. I leaned over onto Eddie's chest and closed my eyes. If this was a bad dream I would just wake up, if it wasn't then I would wake up in the hell that I created by partying at night.

"Where are we?" I asked as I woke up and looked out at a rustic cabin on a lake.

"This is my parents old place," Eddie stated, but I was confused as to why we were there.

"Why am I here?"

"The police department would like a day or two to catch up with Kurt and bring him in for questioning. No one, but Mike knows about this place and he only does because he helped me get the cars off the property without damaging them."

"Who knows we are here?" I asked as my pulse raced with anxiety.

"Some of the detectives, because they will be here with us in shifts, Taylor Cross, Brooklyn, your mom, Mike, and probably a few others, but not many."

"I thought your grandfather left you the cars, not your parents," I questioned everything everyone ever said to me at this moment. My trust fled my body when I opened the box.

"Come here," Eddie pulled me to him and we walked a few steps eastward. "Look where the sun is setting on the hill. Follow it to the trees. The house beside the third tree is my grandfathers."

"I'm sorry," I apologized again. I just seemed to keep screwing up around him.

"It's okay, let me show you the house."

Eddie took me to the door and opened it to let me inside. The hinges cried as he opened the door showing me years of not being used. He flipped on the lights that illuminated a dusty old cabin. There was an old brown couch with two recliners facing a console television that looked like it had had better days.

He held out his hand and walked me into the living room while he dusted some things. When a giant cloud of dust rose from a pillow he looked embarrassed.

"I don't come out here," he groaned. "We will just have to run into town."

Then I watched as he unlocked a gun safe where countless shotguns sat waiting to be used. Then he pulled out a holster and a black pistol. He shut the gun safe door, but never locked it. I guess there wasn't any crime in the middle of nowhere.

"What is that for?" I asked and he frowned.

"To shoot things, make noise, scare people, or anything else you could think of."

"Smart ass," I chided with a smile. "Why are you putting it on?"

"My job is to make you feel safe. This includes scaring off bears."

"Bears?" I shouted. "Where the hell are we?"

"The Catskills," Eddie replied like I already knew.

"Nope, in college I learned there were no grizzly bears, brown bears, or polar bears in upstate New York."

"That is true, but there are black bears. They are essentially harmless, but it is better to be safe than sorry."

"Oh my god," I whined. "I ran away from a killer to get eaten by a bear."

Eddie laughed and escorted me back out the door to the SUV. The two police men climbed inside and drove us into town.

After spending what seemed like a million dollars and buying things I was exhausted again. I had been numb since I saw Brooklyn and it made me tired. On the drive home I fell asleep on Eddie and he merely held me tight.

"Hey gorgeous," he sweetly whispered. "We are here?"

I opened my eyes and saw the cabin filled with evil dust bunnies, and groaned. Steven King would have field day in a place like this.

"I have to crank the generator," Eddie stated as he walked around the side of the cabin and the officers helped me carry in the bags.

I brought out one of the new blanket we had bought and laid it across the dusty couch. Then I climbed on top and fell asleep.

"Brooklyn turn down the radio," I shouted from the couch. "It's too early for that."

I heard nothing over a radio, and had to get my bearings to remember where I was. I looked around and the living room was no longer dusty. It looked like someone had cleaned all night. I sat up and wiped my hand across the log coffee table to feel free oil had been wiped on.

"Morning gorgeous," Eddie stated as he walked in and the screen door closed behind him. "I brought you some grapes."

I nodded my head and walked over to the kitchen where there was a tiny refrigerator with a freezer on top. There was a table set for four, but looked too small to hold more than two. I sat in the wooden chairs and waited as Eddie came in and started cooking.

"How long do I have to stay here?" I asked and he didn't answer. "Can I call Brooklyn?" I asked and he nodded. So I practically lunged for my phone and dialed her number at work.

"Ms. Montgomery's office can you please hold?" Her receptionist didn't even wait for me to answer before pushing the damn hold button. I walked out on the back porch that faced the lake while I waited.

I would admit there were parts of it out here that were absolutely beautiful, but my life belonged in pollution, traffic, and rude people.

"Ms. Montgomery's office how can I help you?"

"Hey Fiona," I spoke into the phone. "Is she available?"

"She is walking over to the courthouse, but we are supposed to patch you through whenever you call. Give me a minute."

Then I heard some dialing and then a ring. I wanted to shout into the phone for her to pick up.

"Brooklyn Montgomery."

"Do you have any idea where I am?" I asked and she laughed.

"Yes, I know where you are, but it is only for a couple days. The judge issued an immediate warrant to pick Kurt up on suspicion of murder and for violating his restraining order. Once they take him into custody bail will be denied and you won't have to see him again."

"Eddie is like all business like in the city and out here he is some kind of farmer who cleans. Oh and there are bears. Did you know there are bears?" I was rambling my problems and Brooklyn was laughing.

"Consider it a vacation, because when you come back you will see its somber here."

"How is my mom?" I asked and I could hear her mumbling to someone to give her ten that I was an emergency.

"Your mom is good. She is thinking of stopping her treatment so she has more time with everyone now that Liza is gone."

I didn't want to talk about it because I would just cry. I should be there right now. Fixing her hair, and dressing her up for a night out with Mike. Helping her get her happily ever after.

"How is the baby?" I asked cause I cared a little.

"She is a fighter. She originally came in at four pounds or just under that, but she is breathing on her own, and healthy. She has to stay in a incubator and wear a oxygen tube, but she is good. Henry is thinking of naming her Rose, after his mother."

"Does she look anything like me at all? Any family resemblance?"

"No honey, remember you farted out of the sky," Brooklyn laughed and I did too.

"Eddie told you about that didn't he?" I asked, but the answer was already there.

"Kate, you are out there for your own protection physically, but if you stop guarding your heart while you are there you might find out whether or not you and Eddie have a future."

"What if the answer is no?" I asked because I was scared he wouldn't be the one for me.

"Then you know," Brooklyn sighed. "Look at it this way. If its not him, then he was your doorway to realize that you didn't want to live the life you were living anymore. He was the angel sent down to show you that you deserved better than what you were giving to yourself."

"Thanks Brook," I gently replied. "You always know what to say."

"The hell I do," She responded sharply. "I read that inside Cosmo just now."

We both burst out laughing and I was feeling a little better about everything.

"Kate, breakfast," Eddie called and Brooklyn heard him.

"He made you breakfast?"

"Eggs, bacon, sausage, French toast, and looks like I have a wide array of fruit," I replied peeking through the window.

"Okay, how about you get him for the weekend and I get him for life?" Brooklyn laughed. "I need to find a new man and move on past Mark," she replied and I knew she missed him. If only he would stop being an ass hat. "Go eat your breakfast and call me later. If there are any updates at all they will let me know."

Chapter 21

I hung up and walked inside. I walked into the kitchen and sat down at the table and began to eat my food. It was so delicious it was hard to keep a straight face.

"You are seriously going to give me nothing?" Eddie asked and I looked at him with confusion as I took another bite. "I can't tell if you love it, hate it, or anything. Your face makes you look constipated."

I burst out laughing and threw a strawberry at him. He threw another back and it landed in my cleavage. He threw his hands in the air and screamed 'Field goal was good.'

"What are we going to do today?" I asked and Eddie started cleaning up his plate.

"I thought I would show you around. Then I have some old vhs movies that should still work, or we can go fishing on the lake. Whatever you want to do," Eddie was being super sweet, and it made me nervous.

I got up and handed him my food as my appetite was only present when we were laughing. Then I walked to the bathroom and closed the door. I climbed out of my clothes and turned on the hot water. Only there was no hot water.

"Eddie," I wrapped the towel around myself and opened the door. "Eddie there is no hot water."

Then Eddie walked around the corner with a look on his face that said he was finding humor in this, but I wasn't going to be happy.

"Darlin'," he said like the south had just rose up and invaded his accent. "Use the lake."

I groaned and then I walked out in my towel and put on the flip flops he had gotten me and I walked out to the lake.

I dropped my towel and dove into the icy water. It was teeth chattering cold.

"Hey," Eddie called out. "You might need this," he shouted and threw me a bottle of baby three in one. Shampoo, conditioner, and body wash that was environmentally friendly. *Oh my god I was in hell.*

I quickly washed, rinse, and swam it out. Then I climbed out of the lake only to get my feet covered in mud. I couldn't win. I grabbed my towel and wrapped it around me as I carried my flip flops to the porch.

I sat in one of the old rockers on the back porch as I picked mud off my feet. Eddie walked out the door carrying a silver tub.

"Put your feet in here," he said and I did as soon as he put it down. I was in Heaven. He washed my feet and gave me a foot rub while I closed my eyes and listened to the birds sing about whatever was happening in their world.

"What the hell was that?" I asked as a muffled bang sounded in the distance. Goosebumps flooded me as I imagined the very worst.

"Honey, there are woods all around us. It is hunting season," he replied and I calmed back down.

"Wait," I shouted when realization came to me. "Where did you get the hot water?"

"I boiled it on the stove and then let it cool waiting for you to get out of the lake."

I sat back in my rocker content with that answer, but he laughed and I glared at him.

"The pilot went out. I re-lit it. In a few hours you will have hot water," he laughed and I threw my towel over his head and pushed him down on the porch as I walked into the house.

I grabbed the bag with the new clothes in it and went into the bathroom. I donned a pink t-shirt that said I was a 'c-u-tie pie,' and a pair of gray sweatpants. I looked ready to be homeless.

I walked out the door to see the officers talking to Eddie. I stopped in my tracks to hear what they had to say.

"Mark says you should let him put her up in a hotel in the city, and to stop listening to Brooklyn," the younger officer said. "Brooklyn said don't listen to Mark he just wants Kate close so he can see Brooklyn," the older one said. I laughed and then walked up to the door.

"Sounds like mom and dad are fighting, so while we are in here fucking why don't you call them to report back and put the phones on speaker and let them yell at each other for a while."

Eddie and the officers all snickered their amusement and then I shut the door in their faces.

"Kate would you like to take a walk with me?" Eddie asked and I looked at the guns. "No bears I swear it."

I nodded and he held out his hand. We walked along the edge of the lake until we came to a curve in it. Then I noticed all these wooden posts with vines on it.

"What's that?" I asked.

"When I was little my parents fought about money a lot. My dad wanted to live on a budget within our means and my mom wanted to drink lots of wine and travel the world buying ugly art. So, when my grandpa gave them half the land he owned my dad built a cabin to live off the land, and my mom climbed up on the hill and planted a vineyard."

"This is a vineyard?" I asked without trying to show too much excitement.

"Yes," Eddie replied and he took my hand and led me over to the vines. He picked a few grapes and walked them over to the water pump and lifted the handle up and then pushed it back down. He did it a few more times and I thought it was dry, but then the water flowed out of it.

He held the grapes under the cold water and allowed them to be rinsed. Then he plucked one off the vine he had picked and brought a grape to my lips. I took it in my teeth and sucked it into my mouth and savored the flavor. These weren't like the ones you got at Trader Joe's these were fresh, juicy, right off the field grapes.

"This is good," I praised the grapes. "I want to take this home with me," I joked. Eddie took off his t-shirt to show me his rippled abs in the sunlight. I understood now why he was built like G.I. Joe, it is because he spent a lifetime working, and continued it in the gym when in the big city. He used his shirt to let me pick a bunch of grapes.

I took my new grapes and wrapped them as we walked back toward the cabin. A hound dog came out of nowhere and started sniffing the grapes in my hands. Then he howled. Eddie walked up and wrapped his arms around me looking down at the dog.

"Bryant you can't have any," Eddie stated and the dog whimpered. "They will make you sick," Eddie tried to tell him no without saying the word, but the beautiful black and caramel hound just tilted his head and barked.

I turned my head to see there was two of them. I laughed when she tried to pry Eddie and I apart with her nose.

"Lily and Bryant meet Kate," Both the dogs barked and they didn't know what for.

"Friends of yours?" I whispered and Eddie nodded.

"They belong to the elderly couple down the lake. I swear to you these dogs are as old as I am if not older. They have been out here since I could walk. They run the whole lake, nothing gets past them does it?" Eddie asked as he leaned down and rubbed their heads.

I laughed and we headed toward the house as the dogs followed us and Eddie made them promises of hot dogs and bologna.

Eddie and I snacked on fruit for lunch and fed the dogs who walked in and out of the back door as if they owned the place for hours. The sun had started to set as we laid on the couch snuggled up watching a old cowboy movie.

Something had been bothering me about my inability to express myself to Eddie. I usually had no filter, but when it came to Eddie and my feelings my lips were sealed. I had to get it out there.

"Eddie," I whispered when his breathing was stable as if he was sleeping. I knew it was now or never. "I wanted you when you brought in the car. I liked you when you stood up for me in the diner. I had grown attached to you when you came and stayed at the hospital during my mom's surgery, but the moment I fell in love with you was on the roof top that night, and I knew it when I saw you taking care of my mom in her hospital room.

"I told Kurt I loved you and didn't even know if I meant it or I just wanted to hurt him. I had never loved anyone before so I wasn't sure, but our time apart showed me that I missed you and it wasn't going away. The ache it left in me was easy to hide because of who I am, but it grew deeper every minute.

"Now we are out here in the middle of nowhere and it terrifies me to let you in because I don't want to wake up back in the city and know it was all a dream. I don't want it to have all been one sided or a lie. I'm terrified."

I moved my arm to wipe the tear from my eyes when I felt lips on my cheek instead. *Damn it I thought he was sleeping.* He turned me into him and held me tightly.

"I care about you a lot more than I should Kate," was the only response I got before we walked into the only bedroom and climbed in the old log bed.

"Brooklyn Montgomery," she answered on the third ring. I was almost afraid I wouldn't get her.

"I hate the hold music," I admitted right away. "Any news?"

"Sorry Kate, they haven't found him, but his team agreed if he shows up for the game they will call the police. That was the whole purpose behind making bail, so if he is not at the game tonight then they will ask Mark and the other guys from the 19th precinct to help out and put it out to the media."

"How is the new job?" I asked and she sounded tired.

"Delayed. Taylor wants me to move in get settled and then join them. I think he is just giving me time to close this up with you. I do have good news though."

"Oh?" I asked cause I wasn't sure what I was going to hear that was good.

"Kurt's lawyer lost the filing to have you charged with prostitution. They cannot say that you were hired to commit the act that day as some form of role play."

"I didn't understand why he would say that," I admitted.

"To make you look like less of a victim to a jury," Brooklyn replied. "How goes it with Eddie?"

"I told him I loved him," I whispered and silence followed. I was sure Brooklyn was laying on a sidewalk dead somewhere in New York

City from a heart attack because the word love left my lips.

"Tell me everything," she said as she told some people around her to shut up and I had to laugh. I told her exactly what I said verbatim and his reaction. Then silence fell again. "I'm so sorry Kate. He seemed so into you I thought for sure it was love."

"It's okay," I quietly replied wiping a tear from my eye. "I wouldn't change a thing except the Kurt stuff if I had to do it all over again. From the first moment when I called him an ass hat, he has been a really good friend and taught me how to find humor instead of anger."

"There is a story for grandkids: I fell in love with your grandpa when I called him an asshat," Brooklyn mocked me.

"Better than saying: I fell in love with your grandpa and let him go because I was a chicken shit," I countered.

We both had our men issues and that was fine, but I needed to get away from Eddie for a while. I needed to clear my head, make adult plans, find a job, and move on. Even with Kurt lurking over my shoulder I would rather leave than stay with a man who doesn't love me back.

Somewhere along the way I had found my self-respect. I had stopped using others like an addict uses drugs. I wasn't partying and I acted like a grown up a lot more. Not all the time, but a lot more. I tried to pinpoint the moment, but I couldn't it just sort of happened.

"Kate," Eddie called and I peeked my head around the corner. "Want breakfast?" He asked and I shook my head.

"I'm going to take a walk up to your grandpa's garage where the cars were if it is okay," I asked hoping for some space, but instead Eddie was getting ready to go with me.

"You stay here, shower, change clothes, and do whatever you need to do and I will be back."

I bolted off the porch wearing my flip flops, sweatpants and t-shirt from the day prior. I had to put distance between us. I needed a fresh start or a new life direction. Something.

By the time I got to the cabin and found the garage Eddie was dripping wet and waiting for me inside.

"What the hell?" I asked as Eddie turned to look at me. The sunlight hit him in the open doors and I bit my lip as the water dripped down his body. "Put a shirt on," I chastised because he was a distraction from what I needed. I wish I had a sponsor for my addiction cause they would be proud here and now.

"Thought maybe we should talk and I heard I needed a shower, so I just swam across the lake."

I looked through the boxes that were in the garage, ignoring shirtless Eddie when I came across an external oil filter.

"This is the one," I said out loud.

"That is the box of parts Mike said we didn't need."

"Before I met you I worked on the Bel Air and I installed one of these. You had the cars I dreamed about, the vineyard I fantasized about, and everything I needed wrapped up in a nice little package with a bow."

"I don't know whether to take that as a compliment or not," Eddie admitted.

I just put the things away and walked out the door. Life has the surreal moments where you don't want to be in them. You don't want to know about them, and most importantly you don't know how to handle them. I was having one now.

"Kate wait," Eddie called out as I got close to the lakes edge. I turned and looked at him as I had finally had my fill.

"I won't wait. You see since I met you my mom was given a death sentence, my best friend yelled at me about being me, my dad called me a whore, and then the Kurt stuff happened, but you want to know what the one thing is that pisses me off?"

"What Kate?"

"You! I want to go home, and you are going to take me and leave me with someone else, because like that car part in there. I refuse to be left in some box to rot when I still have life in me."

Chapter 22

I jumped in the lake in my clothes and started to swim back to the house. I was going to change and leave. My mind was made up and like a stubborn woman nothing was going to change my mind.

At least I thought nothing would change my mind, but then Eddie swim champ from 1995 swam right passed me. So I turned and started swimming back to his grandpas cabin and he started swimming circles around me.

I stopped swimming and just tread water across from him.

"Kate, you can't be mad about last night," Eddie yelled across the water.

"I'm not mad."

"You are the worst liar in the history of women lying. You flair your nostrils, look to the left and blink fast when you tell a lie."

"I'm not lying," I tried to defend myself, but it wasn't working. Damn him for being able to read me.

"Eddie," I started and he cut me off.

"Shut up Kate," he bellowed and it took me by surprise. I expected fear and I think he did too as we both treaded water silently. "I am not going to tell you how I feel when I think you are sleeping. I have balls, big brass ones, that give me the courage to tell you to your face, and I will when you are ready to hear it. Your pathetic attempt to purge me from your system with your confession when you thought I was sleeping won't fix it and I won't act like I heard a word. You have something to say good or bad you tell me to my face Kate!"

I couldn't. I couldn't look into those brown eyes and tell him how I felt. I had never said those words to anyone else so demanding that I say them to his face was just something I couldn't do.

I started swimming and swam past him on the way to the house. We ate in silence. I showered and tried to burn the house down making dinner, even with that there were no words spoken.

I walked out to the hammock as the sun was setting and put my cell phone in my pocket. It was a little chilly wearing just a t-shirt, but I only had the one outfit so we had to wash it after I jumped in the lake.

I grabbed the railing and watched as the light faded and darkness filled the sky. I felt Eddie come up behind me and move my hair to the side. He placed a kiss on my neck and I leaned back into him. He pulled my shirt down my shoulder and kissed the skin that tingled for him.

He gripped my shoulder pulling my skin in a way that had me tilting my head to give him more access. Then just that quickly he spun me and sat me on the railing. He spread my legs and kissed me hard as I held on so I didn't fall.

His fingers moved down to my clit and massage the bud just enough to make me cry out, but no words would leave my lips. I wasn't going to be the one to talk first.

Eddie sensed the tension as I focused on not talking so he dropped to his knees, and looked up at me. Waiting for me to tell him yes or no or fuck me. Whatever the hell he was waiting for he wasn't getting.

He spread my folds and blew warm air across my pulsating apex, and I bit my lip not to say anything. Then he sucked the tight little bundle of nerves into his mouth and gave it a few licks from his tongue. Then as an added form of torture he pulled back and waited for me to break.

I grabbed his hair and moved him back in between my legs hopeful that would be enough, but he merely toyed with me missing everything that was dying for his attention.

"Fuck," I cried out as my frustration hit a new peek.

"That wasn't so hard was it?" Eddie asked and then I knew I had screwed up when he looked up at me and said "beg me."

"Please," I cried out and he began and onslaught that was so fast and slick that I had to use both hands to hold onto the railing or I was going over. I sucked air through my teeth and curled my toes. I was on the precipice when he stopped and stood back up.

I heard a new gun shot, one that was a lot closer this time, but didn't care what animal wandered this way when Eddie was in between my legs. He had an infinite about of energy in that tongue and could stay there all day and night. It was as much a pleasure as it was a curse.

I wanted to run my hands under his white t-shirt and feel his muscles beneath my fingers. I could see his hardened cock through the blue boxers he was wearing. I climbed off the fence and dropped to my knees. Pay back was a bitch.

I pulled him out and licked the crown as I fondled his balls. Then I pulled the head in took it to the back of my throat and swallowed, but I started to choke.

My game had just turned into memory lane and not in the good way.

"Kate," Eddie pulled me up off my knees and held my head while my heart raced. Then he took my hand and we walked around the front of the house and Eddie spoke to the officers.

We climbed in the back of the SUV and we just sat together. I was happy in vehicles; they were my passion so even though this wasn't a classic this was where I wanted to be.

"Are you okay?" He asked and I nodded my head. "Tell me what to do?" He told me to tell him, but that was always the problem. I turned my head and laid a softened kiss on his lips.

"I want you," I explained hoping the words carried the meaning I wanted them too.

He laid me down in the back seat and spread my legs apart.

"I didn't get enough to eat," he growled, but my shaking stopped him and he looked up at me. He eased my fears; "You are so beautiful. I want to make love with you," Eddie spoke out into the darkness. He truly knew exactly what I needed when I needed it, but managed to do it while terrifying me with commitments or things that lead to commitments.

"I'm scared," I finally admitted. "I'm afraid that if I open to you then you will be gone and I will be devastated."

"Kate honey, hear me when I say this. You are a strong beautiful woman. I would want to be with you if you weighed five hundred pounds, with bad teeth, and no hair. Your personality is what makes you beautiful. Open to me and you will see I am not leaving.

"I will be there for you whether you ask for it or not. I will cut through your bullshit and do things to make you smile. I will keep you satisfied, and not longing for anything. You can have all that if you just trust me to give it to you."

"I want to," I whispered, but the fear was there. How could he even ask me for more than just the sex, when I made no promises to him about anything.

"Then try to."

"Would you be more comfortable in the cabin?" I asked and he shook his head.

"No, I think my girl has a thing for cars, new and old, so we will stay right here."

I smiled a huge shit eating grin with his statement as he bent my knee and pushed it against the back of the seat. He put my other foot into the floorboard up against the back of the passenger seat. Then he rose up over me and laid a kiss upon my lips and send cascading goosebumps across my body as he would nibble on my skin, and then kiss it or rub it to make it better. It was an intoxicating combination.

He came to the apex in between my thighs and my pulse raced in my clit as I felt his breath blow on me.

"Lean up, grab the oh-shit handle and don't let go," Eddie growled and I did just that.

In this position if I let go of the handle I would have slid back down in the seat and where Eddie was he would be nibbling on my stomach or something instead of the one piece of flesh that was craving his touch right now. So I tightened my grip.

Eddie parted my folds and I waited with anticipation. He blew air across me and I nearly groaned in frustration, but then like a tiger he dove in to catch his pray.

With the first feel of his tongue on clit my head hit the back window and my grip tightened on the handle. My body screamed to move, to ride his tongue, or anything, but any movement could make me lose my grip or hurt Eddie in the position he was in.

"You taste so good," Eddie spoke up as I tightened the grip on the handle. My clit throbbed so hard I could almost hear it over my heart beat that raced to play along to the rhythm he was setting forth for us.

"Fuck," I called out and Eddie sucked that bundle of nerves into his mouth and slid a finger into me. "Eddie," I cried out because I was losing my grip in the euphoria of it all.

"You let go and I stop," Eddie challenged so I tightened up. I had definitely never done anything like this. He watched as I cried out with an open mouth as another finger got inserted to hit that rough patch of skin that had me screaming out his name.

My mouth stayed open as sounds tried to make their way out, but couldn't. They were trapped underneath the maelstrom of need he had created as he removed his fingers, and replaced them with his tongue.

One of my hands slipped off the handle as I got closer to the precipice. Eddie took notice and climbed up from the floorboard. He moved my bent leg and sat down. Then with a crook in his finger he told me to come to him. I crawled over and climbed up to his lap and began rubbing his hardened cock against my wet pulsating pussy.

I rode him for a few seconds as he pulled off my shirt and threw it over to the other side of the car. Then I grabbed his shirt and threw it as well.

"Stop," he ordered and I halted all movements. "Get a condom."

That was the moment I realized there were none.

"Do you trust me?" I asked and Eddie nodded. "I trust you," I explained as I rose up and positioned him so all I had to do was slide down him.

Eddie seemed hesitant and who could blame him. I was hiding from someone I fucked, but Eddie wasn't like Kurt. He was gentle and gave me what I needed when I needed it.

"I'm clean, on the pill. I'm responsible about that. Every six months-," I tried to explain, but found hands on the back of my neck forcing my head down to kiss him.

This man was as irritating as he a delight. I had fallen down the rabbit hole into what I thought was love. I questioned it, but when he kissed me like I was the only girl he ever wanted to kiss. I was his and I loved him.

He pushed my hips down onto him and my wetness allowed him an easy glide into my pulsating pussy. I placed my hands on his shoulders to help with balance.

"You pick when and I pick where," I repeated. It was what he said about going on our first non-date. He looked kind of confused, so I explained. "I pick how and you pick the pace."

Eddie smiled at my remark, but it fell as I tightened down on him. Up and down, back and forth. I set forth a pattern I knew would drive him wild. I could feel him all over me. His hands never stopped roaming. His lips never stopped finding a new place to kiss.

I shivered when I realized we were no longer fucking. We had moved into making love. Sweat broke out across my body as the windows fogged. My hair grew damp as I continued on relentless rhythm.

"You fit me like a glove," Eddie rumbled out as I leaned back and gave him more of me faster.

"Eddie," I cried out as I felt that pull to my stomach. My heart raced faster, as I leaned in and placed my lips on his. "Eddie," I cried against his mouth as the impending orgasm was going to knock me over.

"Just let go," Eddie demanded, but I was an ornery fool and curled my toes to try and stay it off a little longer. "You fall, I fall, "Eddie grit through his teeth and I felt him swell. I nodded my head and stopped fighting it.

I screamed out his name while the euphoria enveloped me. Electric pulses ran ramped through my body as my entire body tremored and the crashing, debilitating waves of pleasure slammed into me. Eddie rode me down, and then he threw his head back and groaned as he came inside me.

"You okay," Eddie asked as he wiped the sweat from my face.

"I don't – I don't know what to do," I whispered and he looked lost. "No one has ever – how do we clean up the officer's car?"

Eddie looked like he had just conquered a war with the words leaving my mouth.

"Kate, let's be real for a second. I know you have had a lot of sex," Eddie started and I nodded. "You have never let any in bareback?" I shook my head. I started to wonder if there was something wrong with me, until I heard those next six words. "I will be the only one."

"I love it when you talk like something you say will make a new law or something."

Eddie smiled and we used his shirt to clean up. We dumped his shirt in the laundry, I stopped to pee, while Eddie sent the officers somewhere, and then I grabbed a blanket. We headed out to the side of the house where a hammock hung between two trees.

Eddie climbed in first and then I did. Getting in is so much easier than it looks as it sways and plays a game of keep away to keep you out.

I nearly fell out and busted out laughing, but then once I settled in the hammock and found my spot to cuddle into with Eddie I looked across the lake to see the full moon above us.

Eddie covered us with the blanket as the wind rocked us. I leaned up over his chest and looked into those brown eyes that carried that one sliver of green and drove me absolutely insane. I mustered up the courage watching him look at me like I was something special.

"I think I'm falling for you," I whispered and a light smile spread across his face.

"I loved you the minute I met you," Eddie replied and then we made love in the hammock under the moonlight.

Chapter 23

Eddie and I stayed up most of the night talking. We watched the sun rise together and talked about everything. I understood more about why he hated his job and why he wanted to be a paramedic. It explained why he knew me so well and wanted to be there for me. Eddie wanted to be a lifeline to anyone in need, it was embedded in his DNA to be selfless.

He finally drifted off to sleep as the sun rose, but I couldn't sleep. I should have been in euphoria, but questions plagued my mind. Who had been with me when Kurt did that? Who drove him to the hospital and why aren't they stopping him now? Then the one question that was going to be permanently etched into my brain. Why kill Liza?

As I watched him sleep beside me in the hammock I realized I loved him, without a doubt. It wasn't possible this soon, and I didn't understand it, but I knew he was the yin to my yang. Everything I screwed up, he fixed. Every time I got angry, he knew how to calm me down. He had found his way into my heart and it scared the shit out of me.

I turned over and grabbed my phone from the top of the blanket we were beneath. I pushed the power button and watched it light up. As it booted up I realized it wasn't my phone; twelve missed calls from Daisy.

Who the hell was Daisy? Why did I want to kick her ass?

I quickly turned it back off and reached for the other phone and turned it on. I had three messages so I put it to my ear and played them.

The first was from my mom.

"Hey Kate, I hear you are out with the cherry to your coke. I can't wait to call him my son in law. Bring him by for dinner when you get back. I love you, oh this is your mother."

I smiled as I looked down at Eddie, and played with his hair. My mom sounded so happy in the message. I guess we now had dinner plans when we returned.

I played the next message from Brooklyn.

"Kate, I wish I had better news, but Kurt didn't appear at the game. We are putting it out to the media so we can find him and others can take precautions. I truly hope you are out there finding a happily ever after because you deserve it. Call me later, or not if you're getting busy.

Brooklyn was my soul mate, and knew me better than I knew myself. She would go after Kurt herself if she thought it would keep me safe as I would do the same for her. We may not have been sister by blood, but we were family nonetheless.

Then the last one was from an unknown number and at first it was just heavy breathing, like someone jogging or having sex. Then I heard a male grunt.

Tell me Kate, is that why you don't want me? Is it because I didn't eat you? I see you face right now while some guy is in between your legs and you have never looked more beautiful. I can see how much he is enjoying your taste, and want to see how delicious you are myself. I promise when you see me next I will have a taste, or a bite so that my tongue is the last one you ever feel before I cast you into hell with me.

I gasped and my tremors returned for a different reason. I saved the message and turned off the screen and began to look around. Kurt had been here, watching us. I leaned over and gently shook Eddie, and the trees cracked with the movement of the hammock. I wanted to scream out from the noise; I couldn't stop looking around because everything was a new fear. As trees and bushes moved with the winds flowing through the air.

"Eddie," I whispered quickly as panic was setting in, and he turned his head toward me, but his eyes were still shut. "Eddie," I got a little louder and his eyes opened. It took a minute and then I knew he could see the fear in my eyes.

"Kate," he asked, but what could I say. To tell him my past fuck up was out here watching us? I couldn't bring myself to do it. I needed to leave. I needed to see Mark. "You okay?" He asked and my heart shattered, he wouldn't understand, and I couldn't let him in.

"I need you to take me back home now. I need to go to Mark's apartment," I whispered and Eddie looked like he was about to ask a billion questions I couldn't answer. "Please take me to Mark," I begged with panic, needing to get the hell out of here.

Eddie focused on my face and then after a few minutes he got up, walked inside the house grabbing his jeans and slid them on. I climbed out from under the blanket careful to keep myself covered and put my long t-shirt back on while and walked back into the cabin.

"Kate, I don't know what is going on, but I wish you would let me in," Eddie admitted and I nodded. I knew he deserved to know, but this was my problem not his.

"I don't want you to know," I explained in my own way, but it wasn't enough.

"Hear me out for one minute," Eddie went from concerned to angry in his tone. I didn't blame him I would be furious if he kept me out, but this was for his own protection. "I bring you out to my parent's old vineyard to keep you safe, and we make love under the moon, confessing our love, our losses, and our greatest regrets. You open up and finally let me love you, but then you wake me up scared and wanting to go to Marks, and have put up those orange traffic cones closing all roads to you again and you expect me to just do it with no explanation. I deserve to know why."

I merely shook my head to let him know I wasn't going to tell him. We didn't talk for the next four hours, but Eddie held my hand the whole way. I knew he was angry I wasn't being open or honest with him, but I made this mess I couldn't drag him any further into it. I had some kind of dire need to protect what we had built together.

"Can you come to dinner tonight? At my mom's?"

"Are you going to tell me when and where?" Eddie sharply replied. "Cause I would love to say yes, but you seem to only let me in when you want to."

"Eddie," I started, but he cut me off.

"I'm tired of this game Kate. The one where we use each other to scratch an itch, but we sit here and lie through omission to each other. I have tried to be patient, and be understanding. I let you push me away all the time, and hide things from me and now I'm done."

"Eddie," I cried out, but he wasn't finished breaking my heart.

"I love you Kate, and I think I always will. I don't know how the hell it happened and I don't care how, but sometimes when you shut me out loving you is the worst thing in the world and I don't deserve it. I will come to dinner tonight because I care for your mom and I would like to see her. I will smile and act like your boyfriend, but after that I'm done. I can't be in a secretive relationship and I don't want to be. I wanted to be able to share my life with you, but that requires sharing; something you won't do."

I sobbed as I climbed out of the car. I knew this would happen. I knew the minute I let down my guard and opened my heart to him and he would leave me. I fell against the brick wall outside Mark's apartment as the tears overwhelmed my ability to see and an undying need for comfort lingered in the air.

The ache in my chest grew larger as Eddie got in a cab and left leaving me with the two officers who stayed in the car. I tried to dry my tears and take a few steps only to wind up breathless and in a waterfall of my own making. I was dying inside, but fear kept me moving forward.

I finally got to the fifth floor and knocked on Mark's door and when he didn't answer right away I pounded on it in a panic and shouted his name.

"Kate," Mark opened the door looking like he just woke up. "I didn't think you knew what the world looked like this early," Mark joked, but I wasn't laughing instead I burst into tears and wrapped my arms around him.

"What is it?" Mark asked before the door was even shut behind me. He held me tight until I could pull my shit together.

"Eddie broke my heart," I rasped out through more unshed tears waiting to fall. I gasped as saying it out loud made it real. I felt nauseous and wanted to vomit. He was gone, and I had made him leave.

"Why?" Mark asked and then followed up with "I thought you two were perfect together."

"Because," I gasped through the tears. "I wanted you, secrets, and safety, and wouldn't tell him why," I cried as the words all came out wrong.

"Kate, I'm going to be honest I don't speak woman, so I don't know what the hell you are talking about."

"We made love, and then I asked for you, but I didn't disclose why I needed you," I tried again.

"Kate, why did you want me after you had sex?" Mark asked with confusion and disbelief in what I was trying to form. He wasn't there, he didn't understand and I was so hung up on Eddie that I was doing a piss poor job of explaining.

I called my voicemail and pressed play on my messages, but there was nothing there.

How the hell? I know I didn't envision that message.

"Eddie and I went to his parent's vineyard last night and he was there," I explained as I tried to slow my tears.

"Who was there?" Mark asked.

"Kurt," I nearly screamed. "He watched us having sex, and left me a voicemail. I swore I saved it, but I was really shaken up I could have pressed the wrong button."

"Did you physically see him?" Mark asked and I shook my head. "Did you tell anyone where you were going?"

"No, I didn't even know where we were headed. The officers, Brooklyn, and my parents knew where we were."

"So, if he was there he could have followed you over here," Mark rhetorically asked.

"If," I focused in on the one word. "If," I repeated as I got angrier. My emotional overload had hit its capacity so rage was all I felt. "He was there Mark; he knew what we were doing!"

"Kate, I knew what you were going to be doing, and I didn't have to be there. You don't exactly have a celibate record, you know."

"Do you believe me or not?" I demanded an answer.

"I believe you Kate, but I have to ask you this; have you been drinking?"

"No, I haven't had a drink for months I haven't really wanted to since I met Eddie."

My answer floored me. I hadn't even wanted a glass of wine or beer since I met Eddie because I didn't have a need to. He was all I needed and I was going to lose him because of this, and my stupid inability to let him in. *Fucking relationship traffic cones.*

"Okay I am going to get dressed, make a couple calls, and then I am going to follow you as you go home and see if I can catch him in the act. He has an open warrant, so all we need to do is find him. Most of the time when they spiral if we catch them the victims are safe."

"You said most of the time. What happens to the others you don't catch?" I asked with hesitation as the apprehension I felt told me I didn't want to know the answer.

"You don't want to know," Mark replied, but I had to know. He started toward his room and I pulled his arm and made him look at me. "Sometimes predators only stop, when they can't see their prey because they are six feet down in a dirt hole taking a nap in a coffin."

I started shaking and paced the floor while Mark got dressed. I called for a cab, and Mark explained how going ahead of me without the officers would lure him out, and that they would be able to see me in the sea of cabs on our way to my apartment.

I was never the type of person to fear anything, except intimacy and love. This was all new to me and I didn't know how to handle it.

I got out of the cab and ran up the stairs to my apartment as if it were a marathon I really wanted to win. When I got inside I slammed the door and bolted it. I grabbed an umbrella from the stand by the door and peeked around every corner to see if I was alone.

"Kate," Brooklyn called out as she walked around the corner and I nearly stabbed her. "What the fuck," she screamed as I threw the umbrella as adrenaline coursed through me.

"Sorry," I repeated until she could stand there, and look at me normally, and not like she wanted to throat punch me. "I'm a little jumpy." I tried to explain, but it only made it worse.

"Maybe if you told me what the hell you are waiting to attack with an umbrella I could help you and you won't be so edgy."

I had to force my nerves to slow down and explain the whole thing. Then Mike stepped out with a gun from the living room.

Chapter 24

"Mike what the hell are you doing?" I shouted and he looked thru me. Our apartment was covered in boxes from Brooklyn moving out, and Mike was here, but his eyes told me he was somewhere else.

"He got here about a half hour ago and was helping me move boxes," Brooklyn spoke up for him.

"Daddy?" I whispered almost silently as I noticed the dark splatters on his pants. "Dad?" I spoke again as tears filled my eyes, this was all just too much and I needed him to hold out his arms and comfort me, but he was somewhere else.

"He won't bother you anymore," Mike spoke with no emotion. I looked at his blue jean pants again and noticed the splatter was a darkened maroon and it splattered across the top, but pooled at the bottom and covered his shoes. A dreadful feeling coursed through me, and I shook my dead in disbelief.

"Dad, what did you do?" I asked as Mark broke through my bolts and aimed the weapon at Mike.

"He hurt you. I was there, but I couldn't stop him from hurting you," Mike rasped out. "I left him in the park, but they saved him instead of leaving him to die like the other animals."

"It was you?" I asked as shock invaded my core. "You took me to the hospital?"

"Your mom wanted me to pick you up and get some take out to celebrate your new job. I looked everywhere for you and then there was a bang in the speakers, and then I heard-"

"Oh my God," I placed a hand over my mouth as I cried with the realization that when I hit the desk I hit the emergency intercom system and my dad had heard everything he did to me. I cried, and wanted to gag with the memory reel playing in my head. It was bad enough it happened to me, but my dad heard every gruesome growl and groan from the pain.

"No one hurts my baby girl. She deserves the best."

Mark tried to pull me back behind him, but I shrugged him off. Tears filled my eyes as my already broken heart completely shattered. There was blood splatter on my dad's pants, and then I noticed it was on his hands too.

"I have the best, dad, because I have you."

"He should have been punished. I put faith in the system that they would do right by my baby girl, but they let him go."

"Mike, put down the gun, and we can talk about this," Brooklyn spoke softly and he looked over at her with tears in his eyes.

"I heard him he was going to kill my baby girl," Mike explained to Brooklyn and then he turned to Mark. "He was going to rape her and leave her for dead like some kind of piece of trash."

"I wouldn't have let that happen, sir," Mark replied. "I can protect her, but I need you to put down the gun, and tell me where he is."

"Last night, he was going to kill them both," Mike stated with a shaky breath. "Karen went to the hospital and I wasn't there for her because he was going to torture them. I heard him bragging about how it was a two for one special to kill my only daughter and take the life of the man who stole her from him."

"Where is he Mike?" Mark asked again. Tears fell from my eyes as Mike confessed his sins. I wondered how anyone could love someone so much that they would give up their freedom, their life, to keep them safe. Then I realized I already knew because I tried to do the same for Eddie.

"He could be anywhere by now. These two coon hounds showed up and drug him away," Mike replied and I had to smile with mention of Lily and Bryant. Those two trouble makers would make sure no one ever found him.

"Mike, you know they are going to want to take you to jail. As your counsel I advise you not to say anything further, but as your other daughter I say thank you for saving my sister," Brooklyn whispered as she leaned in and placed a kiss on his cheek. "You really are the best dad she could have ever asked for."

"I'm your dad too, Brook, and I would die for each of you. That is my job as a parent. To protect you till the end."

"Daddy," I sobbed. "Aren't you scared to go to prison? To leave mom behind?"

"My sweet baby girl. Your mom and I will be fine. One day we will be together again and I'm not scared of prison. I have lived my life and now it's your turn," Mike rasped out as a tear fell from his eye.

"Daddy?" I asked as he turned pale and looked sick. Sweat broke out across him and the gun tremored in his hand.

"I have protected you, and watched you grow into a beautiful young woman. You are no longer partying, and Eddie is a great guy to step into my shoes and keep you safe. I have loved you your whole life, but now it is time I join your mother to say goodbye."

"Mark," I turned to him and push his hand down with his gun. "Let him go say goodbye to my mom before you put him in prison, please."

Mike looked at me with tears in his eyes. He wrapped his arms around me and let Mark take his gun. I didn't know what was going to happen to him, but I know I would be there all along the way.

"My little Chevy sunshine. Don't ever change for anyone. Don't let anyone steal the light inside you. You are a fighter, not a Found On Road Dead type of girl."

I had to smile with him bringing up a old Ford joke. I was always a bowtie Chevy girl and he would always be the Ford man.

"Maybe I could visit the dark side from time to time and joy ride in a Mustang," I whispered and he squeezed me tighter.

"I would love that," Mike spoke softly as he backed away. Mark read him his rights and placed him in cuffs, and we all left to go to the hospital.

I tried not to think about what my dad had given up for me. I worked excessively hard to not think about the fact that my mom was in the hospital. I even tried not to think about Eddie, but it was all there lurking.

We arrived at the hospital, but the nurses weren't smiling or happy to see us. Nurse Kelly had tears in her eyes and sorrow on her face when she nodded to acknowledge me.

"Miss Huntington," a young doctor called my name and took my hand. Then he began to explain that my mom was no longer my mom. The cancer had moved quickly and invaded her brain. She had drifted off to sleep while I was at the cabin, and wouldn't wake up.

He explained the cancer coma as a trip down memory lane. That I was to talk to her and let her remember all the good times because even though she couldn't wake up and see me that she could still hear me. That the hearing was the last to go so I was to say everything I needed to.

"Baby girl," Mike called out as Mark released him from his cuffs and I turned to Mike and held on tight as the news stole my air and my brain spiraled that I would never be able to talk to her again. "She is going to a better place where there is no more pain, no more illness, and she can watch over you."

"I want her to stay," I cried as my world once again tilted on its axis and my lifeline was leaving. "I know she is in pain and I am a selfish bitch, but I can't help but want her to stay with me."

Mike held me tight as sweat poured off of him, and he fumbled with his words.

"It is not selfish to want her to stay. It is only selfish if you make her stay. Let her go, baby girl. Let her pester you about son in laws and babies from Heaven where there is no more cancer. Let her pass on without any regrets."

I let go of Mike and turned my attention to Brooklyn as I cleared my throat and tried to stop the flow of tears. I watched across the room as the doctor spoke to Brooklyn and handed her a folder with my name on it.

I pulled myself together and we all walked into the room. I saw my mom hooked up to machines, and tubes. There were lines running in and out of her everywhere, and she was translucently pale. You could tell she was barely holding on, but fighting to live. I could feel her energy around me.

We all took a seat while I tried to think of all the things I wanted to say. Brooklyn opened her folder and looked over something and then smiled. She walked over and leaned down and whispered in my mom's ear.

"You know that favor you asked of me, Karen. I think you will love the outcome," Brooklyn spoke sweetly and then she began reading some form. I ignored it for a bit and then I had to do a double take, and make her repeat a part. "According to the DNA provided by Henry Huntington he cannot be Kate's biological father. Michael Andrew Kelsey congratulations you are a dad. She is 99.9% yours."

I watched as Mike sobbed tears of joy and I read the paper. I grabbed onto Mike and hugged him tighter than I ever had before.

"I always wanted it to be you," I whispered and he laughed.

"Kate, it was always me. Didn't matter where you came from you were always mine."

"Why?" I asked when I let go of Mike and turned to Brooklyn smiled. I was going to need to buy stock in Kleenex with the day I was having.

"Your mom didn't want to leave you with a tyrant. She had hoped you were Mike's because of all the things you had alike, but even more so the way you clicked. You came out six weeks early which is why she thought you belonged to Henry."

I turned in my chair and wrapped my arms around Mike once more. He really was the dad I had wanted all along, and this was the best thing my mom could have ever given to me.

I stepped out of the room and went to the bathroom to blow my nose when Nurse Kelly came in.

"Kate," she whispered. "I'm not supposed to give you time lines because we don't always know everything, but if you have any family that needs to come and say goodbye you need to call them now."

"Why?" I asked as my new elation exited my soul and despair moved in.

"The death rattle," she answered, but I didn't know what she meant. "You will hear it when you walk back in there. It is how we know they are down to hours. I'm so sorry."

Nurse Kelly pulled me into a hug as a new type of grief flooded me. When she walked away I picked up the phone and I called Eddie at work.

"Mr. Wellington's office, this is Daisy, how can I help you?"

"Daisy?" I questioned. This was the woman who kept calling Eddie and demanded to be put through to him. Who the hell was she? Was I allowed to ask?

"This is Kate Huntington, and I need to speak with him it is an emergency," I replied and she blew a bubble gum bubble and popped it in the ear piece.

"Unlike some people I will follow procedure and put you through."

"Hello Miss Huntington," he spoke formally as if I meant nothing to him at all.

"I need you at the hospital, a lot has happened and -,"

"Kate," he cut me off with a sigh. "I am getting ready to head out for drinks with the guys although I don't know why I am telling you since you share nothing with me. If you still need me come midnight you know how to make a booty call right?"

"Eddie she's dying," I shouted, and he let out a rush of air.

"I'm sorry Kate, I really am, but you chose not to make me part of your life. I can't be that stuffed animal you hug every time you need something to hold and toss in the floor when you don't want me anymore."

"Eddie, please, I need you," I cried into the phone and he stayed silent on the line and then with an exasperated groan he hung up."

I cried onto the floor as all my lifelines left me one by one. I thought this was it, the end of me, but my mom would have been so disappointed if I had given up so easily.

I picked myself up, and pulled my hair into a ponytail holding it up with a pen that Nurse Kelly had dropped. I fixed the white button down long sleeve shirt that I had stolen from

Eddie and looked like I had slept in, and brushed the dirt off my jeans.

Then I grabbed some tissues and stuffed them in my pockets, just in case, and headed for my mom's room.

I was going to say goodbye.

Chapter 25

"Do you remember when I was little and I swung the swing too high and you told me to stop, but I didn't listen. I lost my grip and flew right into that tree. That was the moment I learned I should always listen to you."

I was leaned over holding my mom's hand drowning out the sound of her rattled breaths that screamed of darkness with memories that would make her smile.

"How about when I was seven and I was in the beauty pageant. I didn't want to wear a bathing suit in front of the boys in the audience so you put on a two piece to match mine and walked out with me. That was the moment I knew was courage was."

Mike ran his hand across my back in comfort. Mark had said his goodbyes, and left him with a guard at the door because the police chief forced him to head upstate and help them find the body.

"Do you remember when I got sick and threw up all over the car we were test driving? I look back and laugh at it now that you got him to come down seven thousand dollars on the car and then chose one in a different color I hadn't thrown up in. That was the moment I learned how to finagle, and have been doing it ever since."

Brooklyn walked in with a cup of coffee for me and Mike as we all gathered round my mom for her last moments with us.

"I won't remember you like this, mom, I will remember you healthy and wholesome. I will remember the laughter and tears. I will remember Brooklyn and I running from you when it was time for a spanking, or helping at the diner when you were just too beat to do it alone. As long as I live I will remember everything you gave up for me, and everything you gained from me. I am thankful for the time we got together and the lessons that I learned. I am elated to know that the man I wanted to be my dad, was him all along, so I am even grateful you got knocked up and kept me, but most of all I am so proud that you were my mom. I was blessed with the best, and nothing will ever change that."

My mom started taking long deep breaths and holding it as Nurse Kelly came in and looked at her monitor. She nodded her head and I held my mom's hand. This was it, my mom was dying. I thought I would be overwhelmed with grief, and I was, but I was able to keep it back to say goodbye.

"I love you, Karen," Brooklyn cried as she held her other hand.

"Go now my angel, and find us a place in Heaven. I will see you soon," Mike spoke softly as leaned over and placed a kiss on her forehead. He was nearly green and I wondered how he was holding up with all of this, but I would deal with it after she had left us.

"Your mom and I have already said our goodbyes. This is between you and her now," he whispered as he stepped out to go use the bathroom down the hall.

She took another deep breath and held it and I looked at the Nurse who gave a look telling me it was time to say goodbye. How the hell do you say goodbye forever? What do you use as the last words they ever hear?

Then I knew, I leaned up and placed a kiss on my mom's head and sang softly into her ear.

"I'll be cherry and you be coke, cause no one needs a root beer float. As long as I have you and you have me together we will be sweet as iced tea. Sing out loud and give it a whirl, no one can defeat a soda pop girl."

My mom let out her breath she had been holding and didn't take another. Nurse Kelly muted the screen as I stood over my mom and said goodbye.

"I love you. You will always and forever be the cherry to my coke. Go to Heaven and wait for me at the pearly gates. Go boss God around about a having son in laws and babies for a while."

Then she was gone.

I was in a tunnel. Nothing around me seemed to exist, there was only her and I. I took a deep breath as I felt her presence dwindling from around me.

"Goodbye mom," I whispered and closed my eyes as my hand held hers until she was cold.

There was a huge commotion that broke that moment of loss I had fallen into and turned my attention to the door. Brooklyn stood up and walked to it and pulled the door back and I walked up behind her to see the staff working on Mike on the floor.

I ran and slid on my knees to get to him as they put a mask over his face and did compressions on his chest. I screamed 'save him' and heard them tell me to move. The orderlies brought up a gurney and they counted to lift him up off the floor and get him into a room where they could try to revive him I sat up against the nurses' desk and cried.

Brooklyn came to me and held me while they all shouted orders around us. Two lifelines in the span of five minutes left me debilitated and alone. Everything suddenly went numb and I couldn't feel the pain anymore, or the shouting. I merely heard the sound of something plastic hitting the floor.

I looked and a pill bottle had fallen from Mike's hand and clattered on the floor near us. I leaned forward and grabbed it feeling like everything was happening in slow motion. I looked at the prescription label that had been torn off and instead in pen was written 'for my daughter.'

I opened it to see a thick piece of paper folded inside. With shaky hands I opened it as everything around me faded. I had tunnel vision and it was only focused in on the letter:

I know I should have left you more than a note, or an explanation of why I felt like now was an okay time to join your mother. You see when she got sick I knew I couldn't leave you alone, and then I met Eddie one night and knew he was the one for you.

Arrogant and cocky, but full of laughter and always wanting to help people. He was the black to your white. The rainbow to your pot of gold. You would have never let your mother and I set you up so we did what we had to do.

I wiped out my 401K with the company which is why Henry firing me didn't matter. You see we had already discussed it prior when I emptied my retirement. I bought the cars and placed them out at Eddie's grandpa's garage. I knew Eddie would find them when he was ready to say goodbye to his family I just had to wait and hope he did it before your mom passed on.

I picked your three favorites so that you would always have a piece of me with you. You will find the titles signed over to you taped under the coffee table in your apartment. Then when the time came and I saw you with Eddie at the hospital. The sparks flew between the two of you, and I knew it was a match made in Heaven.

I never asked him to come and stay with us while your mom had surgery. He did that because he had already found his soul mate. He just didn't know it yet. We men are hard headed and do things we don't understand until we see the whole picture. He was a goner the minute he met you, because you were perfect for him.

Your life was headed into a chaotic long and lonely life like your mother had and she didn't want that for you. So we might have brought you two into each other's lives, but look at what you have become since you met him. You don't drink. I don't have to wonder where you are at 4am. You can go grocery shopping without worrying you will run into a one-night stand because you don't notice them anymore.

You have more sass in your little finger than your mother had her whole life and I blame Brooklyn and thank her for making you that way. So the only things that changed were the things you were already unhappy with, but didn't know how to stop.

I gave you Eddie and he gave me back my daughter. When your mother took a turn for the worse we had a conversation about the end of times, and made an agreement that if you were happy, safe, strong enough to survive our loss, and you could laugh again, I would join your mom. I did that, Kate.

Your mother made you strong enough. We all did our part to keep you safe, but Eddie made you laugh again and that made you happy. Brooklyn and Mark had a role in there too, but they have to find their own way as you have found yours.

I couldn't save Liza, but we were able to save you. When Eddie walked into a room you lit up like a beacon for him to see, and I knew that you would be okay without us. I often wonder if you saw your mother and I that way.

I don't want tears, or sappy goodbyes. Save those for your mom because she deserves them. I want you to celebrate my life. Go get a drink, just one, with Brooklyn and start your new life with a clean slate.

I have always been and will always forever be your dad. I love you more than life itself, but we made you strong enough to survive on your own without us. This is our time now to be together. I know this hurts and I am sorry, but know that I am so happy because whatever happens when you die I won't do it alone. I'm headed to our afterlife with your mother."

My lifelines, most of them anyway, were gone. I looked up at the clock that stroked twelve, and wanted to give it the finger.

My mom was gone, my dad was gone, Kurt and Liza were both gone as well. Everyone I knew good or bad were leaving me for the afterlife and for a split second I couldn't help but want to join them.

"Kate," Brooklyn cried as she held onto me. She had now lost two mothers and I was selfishly thinking about walking beside my mom after losing just one.

"They want a celebration," I murmured as I pulled every ounce of strength I had from some unknown place just to get up off the floor.

"Miss Huntington," the doctor came to me with that solemn look they give you when they feel defeated in their chess game with death. "I'm so sorry," he whispered as he placed a hand on my shoulder. "We did everything we could," he continued and I nodded to each remark.

"My dad is with my mom, and that is where they want to be," I replied softly as I held the letter tightly in my hand.

"You okay? I can prescribe you something to help over the next few days until Monday and then you can see your regular doctor," the young doctor asked, and it was a crutch. I could take it, but then the pills would become replacements for sex and alcohol I had once needed to cope. People with addictive personalities like mine needed to steer clear of things like that.

"No, I will be fine," I whispered as sorrow filled my soul and wondered if it was a lie.

"We need to make arrangements," I said to Brooklyn as she led me to the elevator. I pushed the button to go up another floor and Brooklyn wiped her tears to look at me crossly, but said nothing.

I took her hand and we exited the elevator and walked down the hallway. There we came to a window where Henry was rocking a new baby in his arms as tubes came out of her like my mother had had.

I knocked and he waved at me to come in.

"Kate," he finally got my name right. "I would like you to come and meet Karen Rose Huntington. Your sister," Henry showed me the tiny little baby and I asked if I could hold her. I sat in the rocker and the nurses helped transfer her from him to me.

She was so tiny and fragile, and the need to protect her and teach her to be strong filled me as I watched her little fragile body snuggle into me.

"I know you're not my daughter. I got the same paperwork this morning, but I would like to get to know you. I would like to try this again without force or strain."

"I think I would like that," I replied softly as baby Karen yawned in my arms. "Why did you name her Karen?" I asked out of comfort.

"I know I have been obstinate and awful, but there was a time before you where I could be a lot of fun. I met your mom in the prime of that, and she was the one who got away. I gave her everything and she just left me there by a fire in the woods during a rock festival. I named her Karen because I want her to grow up strong, independent, and confident. The three qualities Liza lacked and Karen had in spades."

"I think she will grow up to be just fine, as long as you don't buy her fake tits," I laughed and baby Karen opened her eyes to look at me. "Hi little one. Your dad here is a grumpy old man, but I think he will take amazing care of you. In fact, I know he will because there is an angel named Karen who just entered Heaven and will be in need of someone to watch over. I bet she picks you just so she can throw things at your daddy. My mom and dad are in Heaven with your mommy and they will all keep an eye on you little one."

I looked up at Henry to see tears in his eyes, as I just told him my mother had died. He turned his back to me so I wouldn't see the sadness and I looked back down at baby Karen.

"Brooklyn you have to make me some babies with Mark," I smiled as she watched me with baby Karen. "I know it's a tall order, but what's a one-night stand when you get a lifetime of love from a tiny little baby."

"You want Mark's babies, you go have them," she laughed through her tears.

"Is that permission?"

"No," she shouted defensively. "He's still mine, even if he doesn't realize I exist. One day I hope he loves me as much as Karen and Mike loved each other."

"He already does," I replied as the nurse came and took the baby for a feeding.

I walked over and wrapped my arms around Henry and whispered in his ear.

"She loved you in her own way, if she didn't she would have never hunted you down and thrown me at you."

"She was definitely a stubborn woman when she thought she was right," Henry replied. "I would love for you to stay and work with me at the office, but something tells me your heart is not in it."

Henry leaned back and pulled keys out of his pants. I watched as he took three off and handed them to me.

"What is this?" I asked and he closed my hand around them with an emotional smile.

"I think this might help right a wrong. These are the keys to your garage. I'll send the paperwork over in a couple weeks. You ran it better than I ever could, and Mike and I wanted you to have it."

"I can't-," I tried to refuse, but there was no telling him no. Brooklyn came up and linked her arm in mine and led me out of the room so Henry could compose himself better.

I had loved and lost.

I had lost and loved.

I had lost my heart and gained a new bigger one that was capable of loving openly and easily.

Chapter 23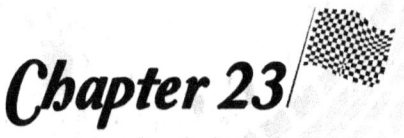

Six Weeks later

"I am calling from outside the house," I spoke into the phone.

"I am answering from inside the house," Brooklyn replied as we both laughed.

We made plans to unpack her new apartment with Chinese food, wine, and a movie. I headed out in a cab and went and picked everything up. Then I got to her new apartment to see the door was open. I peeked my head around the corner and looked to see her looking at Mark the way my mom used to look at Mike as he spun her in the air.

I decide to stay hidden in the nook and watch them interact. I could almost feel the spark between them, and had to wonder if that is what Mike meant when he said he saw it between me and Eddie.

"I am a detective. You didn't have to," Mark replied to Brooklyn about something with a smirk on his face.

"So, what you're saying is that you're a legal stalker?" She sharply retorted as she walked up to him.

"I am whatever you want me to be when you look at me like that," Mark replied and I wanted to just put up a big neon flashing sign that said here is your chance for Brooklyn.

Mark lifted her off the floor in a bear hug. I was about to make my entrance, but then a song came on her IPod that took me back to memories of when they first looked at each other the way they were looking now.

"Do you remember the first time we danced to this?" Mark asked Brooklyn.

"I do, we were having oldies night at the school and Kevin had just dumped me. You held me in your arms and danced with me all night. You saved me from myself that night," she replied forgetting that Mark had to go into the bathroom and drag her out with a tear stained dress. *At least I remembered it accurately and not in the romantic way she did.*

"I've missed you, Mark," Brooklyn said softly and I wanted to alert the world that my sister had found her cojones, and told him, okay kind of told him how she felt, but then I saw the look on his face and she wasn't going to like the response so I stood up.

"Hey, Kate," Brooklyn said hi as Mark let her go.

"Hi, Kate." Mark stated as he acted like nothing was knew.

"Hey, guys. I brought Chinese food and I have three bottles of wine. Who is ready to watch Jack Ryan: Shadow Recruit?".

"Mark would you like to stay for dinner?" Brooklyn asked and I was a little irked that she would ask him since this was supposed to be a girl's night.

"Did you get any General Tso's?" Mark asked as he took my bags into the kitchen.

"I sure did, because I knew you would be here," I stated with sarcasm.

"Shh, Kate, no one is to know I was here," Mark replied as he waved his hands around like he was hypnotizing me.

"When will you stop these childish games and make a woman out of me?" I asked with humor as my mood had just lightened.

"When you start bringing me Chinese food and my slippers," Mark replied and I faked a southern scoff.

"She got the General Tso's because it is my favorite, but I share with hot guys and policemen," Brooklyn spoke up and I giggled because I knew where this was going.

"What category do you put me in?" Mark asked as he tickled her.

I watched as Brooklyn pressed her body against his and dropped to her knees slowly and then placed a kiss on his belt. I think I was going to vomit if they started screwing in front of me. So I took a swig from the bottle of wine I had already opened in the cab;

"When my body against yours starts affecting you, then I will add you to the hot guy column. Until then, you get to stay off that list," Brooklyn sweetly spoke to Mark.

"That was cruel, woman!" Mark bellowed and I laughed.

"You could be Chris Pine's doppelganger," I shouted and held up the movie case to Mark's face. I was feeling a little tipsy, but having fun basking in the electricity between the two of them.

"Did you open the wine in the cab on the way here?" Brooklyn asked and I nodded, but I couldn't miss the disappointment on her face. It was just one bottle not like I had a strange man in my hoo-ha right now.

Brooklyn took my hand and led me to the couch as she said goodbye to Mark. I didn't hear what she said, but he looked hurt. I wanted to know, but at the same time I didn't want to dive into their story.

"What?" She glared at me.

"You got it bad."

"What are you talking about?" Brooklyn asked as if I had to tell her.

"You want him. You need him. You love him," I turned it into a little song that was annoying to get stuck in your head.

"We are just friends," Brooklyn told me her first lie.

"Yeah, because friends refuse to call each other. You two must be such great friends that you can communicate through telepathy. You both know you haven't come around since he started dicking it to that one chick."

Brooklyn rolled her eyes with a scoff and tried to walk away. I pulled her arm and became the friend to her that she had always been to me.

"Look, stick the moral compass in your purse. He wants you. You want him. Now jump on his grill chest and get it out of your system before you explode and start dating a vibrator."

She shook her head as I gave her my biggest smile and then she rolled her eyes. She would see I was right, she just needed some time.

"His grill chest? What does that even mean?" Brooklyn asked.

"You remember my last cookout? Remember that grill I borrowed? The grate was rock hard and made of steel. I imagine his chest would look like that with line after line of rock hard abs. I also think that if I I climbed on top of his chest I would get burned because he is so hot."

I faked fanning myself as she rolled her eyes and went into the kitchen and made us plates, turned off her Ipod, started the movie and sat down with me.

"How are you doing, really?" Brooklyn asked and I sighed.

"The days following the funeral were rough. I didn't even know that Eddie came until my mom's cousin Martha talked about how wonderfully delightful he was. Then the silence fell. You had moved out, my parents were dead, Henry is struggling now that baby Karen is home and she doesn't want to sleep and doesn't like her nanny. So I was alone in my apartment not wanting to burden anyone, and I picked up a bottle."

"Kate, you were never an alcoholic so there is nothing wrong with having a drink," Brooklyn tried to make me feel better.

"When I woke up I was still alone and the quietness was my undoing. I threw out all my alcohol. I threw out my condoms," I stated and Brooklyn gasped.

"What about safety first?" She asked.

"I'm gonna save my cookie for the right guy instead of the next guy."

"How is the garage?" Brooklyn asked and I smiled really big.

"It's amazing. Henry set me up with a financial guy and it turns out Mike was turning over two million a year working on the classics. People would ship them in just for him to work on them and now that they know I am his daughter they are asking me to fix them too."

"That sounds great," Brooklyn gave me a half grin. I knew she was worried about me getting in over my head.

"I'm going to pay it forward," I told her and her face scrunched in confusion as she pushed her black hair off her shoulder. "I gave the address of the shop to ten homeless men that I have remembered being on the street from when I was little. Most of them were veterans so they have understanding of how to fix stuff. I'm holding workshops every weekend where they can come out and stay the night. I feed them and they learn a skill set."

"That is wonderful, Kate, but are you safe?" She asked and I merely nodded. I didn't think any of those guys would hurt me, but until someone tells you everything do you really know anyone?

"I will never understand men," Brooklyn said out of the blue about half way into the movie.

"Me neither," I replied and took another drink. "I shouldn't be drinking this, but it makes it easier."

"Makes what easier?" Brooklyn asked.

"Life, love, loss, and whatever the hell else is out there."

"Is this about your parents or Eddie?" She asked and I just looked at her. "I haven't said it because your parents died, but I am gonna say it now. So buckle up sweetheart this might hurt a little," Brooklyn started.

I took another swig and sat the bottle on the coffee table with my plate and turned all my attention on her.

"I would have left you long before Eddie did. You were angry, obstinate, selfish, a cock's best friend and you held in stuff better than half the priests I know. I love you so I say this with all the love in my heart, you are angry with him for not being there when you needed him, but where the hell were you when he needed to be let into your life?

"You expected him to be the one thing he could never be," she finished and took a drink of the wine.

"What pray tell might that be?"

"A fucking mind reader, Kate!"

Chapter 24

The next morning, I was completely exhausted and hung over. I think I might have been able to sleep it off had I been at home, but I was glad I stayed at Brooklyn's, the case they put her on was the same one I feared they would and she was having nightmares about it.

I rode out to the cemetery and put new flowers on my parent's graves. I had them buried side my side into one hole, so there was no dirt between them. They had waited their whole lives to be together so when the mortician said he could build a box to let their coffins lie right beside each other I was all over it.

Baby Karen got to go home from the hospital a few weeks ago. Henry would bring her out and he would talk to my mom and even my dad. I think he felt like things were left unsaid between my mom and him, but she had no regrets so he needed to let his go. I finally put a bench beside their graves so that he didn't have to sit on the ground.

I sat at the foot of their graves and picked at the grass. I watched as the sun shined brightly down on the river, and took a deep breath before confessing my feelings to a tombstone hoping my parents could hear me.

"Daddy, I think I screwed up and let Eddie go because of fear, but I am so angry that he didn't stay. I am furious he didn't fight harder or come when I needed him the most. I started drinking again and had I not been with Brooklyn last night I would have been in the bar falling into old habits, and not because of loneliness this time, because I don't want to feel the pain anymore. I'm hollow without him and no drink can fill it. I don't know what to do. Give me a sign," I begged.

I laid in the grass and watched the clouds roll overhead. It was something I had seen a little blond girl do when I was little. She would lay next to the tombstone and call out the shapes of the clouds when she ran out of things to say to whoever she was missing. I put my sunglasses down and called out the shapes as well until I fell asleep.

"Kate," a familiar voice called out. "Kate," I heard it again. I sat up, but it was merely my mind playing tricks on me because there was no one out here. I laid back down just in time to hear a crash nearby. I sat up again with a jolt and saw a 1957 Chevrolet Bel Air and a dump truck had collided.

I ran down the hill as someone else went for the driver of the classic car. I slid over the top of the car and popped the hood up. I immediately disconnected the battery, wiring harness, and anything else I could think of that would cause a spark and lead to a fire.

When I lowered the hood back down I looked in the window to see Eddie in the back seat holding a woman's head and talking to her little boy.

The dump truck driver was on the phone with emergency services. I asked him if he was all right, but he waved me off. I ran over to the car and opened the front passenger door.

"How is everyone in here?" I asked and the mom whimpered in pain while Eddie held her neck firmly against the seat.

"I'm fine, how are you?" A little voice called from the back seat. I leaned over and looked down to see her son didn't even have a scratch. He was playing with two dinosaurs in his car seat and was oblivious as to what was happening.

"What is your name?" I asked the little boy.

"I'm Michael, but my mom calls me Mikey," he said proudly, and I internally thanked my dad for the sign from above. Here Eddie and I were working as a team to help this little one and his mom. The yin to my yang.

"Let's see if we can get your mommy some help," I said and looked to Eddie.

"I'm holding her neck in place until emergency services gets here. In case she has had a spinal injury we have to keep her immobilized. See if you can see any other injuries.

I looked down to see a nasty gash in her leg from the steering wheel.

"I'm going to have to take the steering wheel off to see if there is anything in the wound."

I worked my magic and pulled the steer wheel off with a screw driver and a pair of wire cutters I had found under the seat. Eddie talked to Mikey who was asking why they call grown up talks birds and bees.

As soon as I lifted the steering wheel I saw that the door handle had impaled itself into the muscle of her calf and then the wound began bleeding profusely.

"Eddie," I called out as adrenaline took over my actions, but I didn't know what to do. He looked over the seat and saw the blood, but couldn't let go of her head.

"Take my belt off and use it as a tourniquet."

I climbed over the seat and sat between Mikey and Eddie. I fumbled getting his belt off because of the close proximity to Eddie. My hands shook and I was anything but calm as nausea rose up and I looked forward to see the blood soaking her clothes.

"Kate," Eddie used that voice that demanded attention. "Listen to me. Take a deep breath for me," I did exactly as he said. "Close your eyes and pull off my belt without anything else in your view."

I got it off and opened my eyes to see everything a little calmer. I was still panicking, but Eddie's eyes told me everything would be fine. I climbed back over the seat and tried to lifted the woman's leg to put the belt under it, but she was stuck.

"Eddie, I can't get it," I cried as more blood poured out.

"Hold her completely still. Place your hands where mine are and hold her here."

"What is your name?" I asked as I moved to hold her like Eddie had.

"Karen," she finally told us as she pleaded with God to save her. I cast a look to the sky and murmured 'enough signs dad' and then focused on her. Eddie and the dump truck driver with the help of another pedestrian that had just ran up on the scene pulled the door open and they were able to pry her leg lose.

They lifted her leg and wrapped the belt tightly above the wound. She screamed in pain as they tightened it again to stop the bleeding. She arched herself forward, and with the blood on my hands I lost my grip, but Eddie had seen it coming and placed his hand over her throat to help hold her in my hands.

Emergency service finally got through the traffic and I had my tow truck driver, Bob, come and pick up the car. I promised Karen and little Mikey I would have it good as new in a few weeks.

I wiped the blood onto my white summer dress and walked over to Eddie.

"Hi," I spoke softly.

"Hi," he replied as he looked at me. I could still see how he felt in his face, but he had a thick wall up and there was no way I was getting past his guards unless he let me. "Thanks for the help in the car," he replied and looked like he was going to walk away.

"What are you doing out here?" I asked as this was not his side of town.

"Remember when I told you that you were my second chance to save someone worth saving," he replied and I nodded my head. "My fiancé is buried up on the hill not far from your parents. She was worth saving, but I wasn't there when she needed me and now she's gone."

He had opened the door and gave me an inch, now it was on me to open up and let him in.

"I'm sorry Eddie, I didn't know," I replied in a hushed tone.

"You never let me in, so I never shared," he shrugged and turned to walk away.

"Where is your tie?" I asked noticing his jeans and Yankees t-shirt.

"I quit," he responded as if I should know what he was talking about.

"Why?"

"I didn't want to be the type of person who spent any amount of time doing something I didn't love. Life is too short for that."

"Is life to short to forgive me?" I asked and he turned back to face me. "I'm really sorry I shut you out. I shouldn't have, but even though I screwed up you should have been there for me. You should have spanked my ass red, or something, but you should have been at the hospital when they -," Eddie cut me off.

"I was there, Kate, I watched from the waiting room while you sat in the floor reading a piece of paper. I watched as everything that made you you evaporated before my eyes. I saw you slink back inside yourself. I wanted to be there for you, but you didn't need me there."

"You're wrong!" I shouted as tears welled up in my eyes. "I don't give a damn what you saw because I needed you. I wanted you to hold me and tell me it would be okay. I needed you to love me and not leave me feeling like my world had ended," I sobbed and Eddie walked up and pulled me into his arms.

"I'm sorry," he whispered over and over again. "I'm an ass-hat Kate, and I'm sorry."

"Don't you ever do that to me again," I cried as I pounded on his chest. "They are gone, and I can't bring them back."

Eddie held me on the side of the road for nearly and hour with murmurs of apologies, and laughter outshining the tears. It was so easy to forgive him, but so hard to forget. I had to decide then and there if I wanted a future with him, and make the commitment I found so terrifying.

"I'm going to dinner with Brooklyn tonight, do you have plans for Sunday?" I asked hopeful he would say yes.

"Why don't you go get cleaned up, and I will go get cleaned up. I can pick up some Thai and meet you at the garage. I know you need to file the accident quotes with the insurance company. So, you can talk, eat, and work all at the same time. Maybe even teach me how to rebuild a carburetor for this older Cadillac I am looking to buy."

"Maybe we could just give it a few days and see where we are. You know you want me to multi-task and I can't?" I hesitantly stated with a fake smile as my head swirled with thoughts of babies and marriage. "You know why I don't ever eat gum? Cause I will trip and fall on my face."

"I'm gonna go, Kate," Eddie called out and I let him start to walk away. He turned a corner and I shouted his name. When he stepped back he turned to look at me and I swallowed all my fears.

"Two hours Eddie, don't be late or I won't let you in," I replied hoping he took it as I intended it to mean.

Two hours later on the very minute I had a knock on my garage door. I opened the door and Eddie walked inside with a bag of take out.

I took the blanket and grabbed his hand; leading him outside. Then there by the cherry tree where my mom and dad reconnected I had a picnic with Eddie.

"I missed you," I stated with a mouth full of noodles.

"Okay, we covered the looking at me when I am awake and talking to me, but not with food in your mouth," he replied and I laughed as I covered my mouth.

"I missed you," I tried again after I swallowed. "I want to apologize to you for being awful, but you started it by being an asshat," I smiled.

"You just apologized and then insulted me, you owe me one more apology," Eddie stated and I grabbed his black t-shirt in my hands and pulled him over to me. I sucked his ear lobe into my mouth and then kissed his neck.

"You are sorry," I breathlessly said after I saw his cock harden in his jeans. He pushed me onto the ground and quickly lifted my blue jean skirt.

"No panties," he growled as he pulled my legs apart and sucked my clit into his mouth. I didn't care that we were out here on a hilltop overlooking the Hudson. I didn't care that anyone could drive up and see us. As I wove my fingers into his hair and moaned when his finger entered me the only thing I cared about was making sure he reached the finish line with me.

"I take it you forgive me?" I breathlessly asked as he pushed another finger in.

"I could ask you the same," Eddie replied and then we smiled at each other and the hurtful past was put in a box of thing to never remember. He dove into my apex and flicked his tongue in that way I had come to love.

I pushed his head up and sat up. He looked at me weirdly, but I pulled his black shirt off, and unfastened his jeans.

"Lose them," I ordered.

"You first," Eddie challenged.

We both stripped down completely naked and I pushed him onto his back on the blanket. Then I crawled up and place a kiss on his lips.

"I wasn't done with you," he called out and I smirked. I wasn't nearly done with him either, but I still had one more thing to overcome. I draped my body across his with my pussy in his face and his cock throbbing angrily wanting to go in mine.

"You don't have to do this, Kate," he spoke sweetly and it warmed my heart.

"Let me do this. I need to do this. As long as I can't I am still his victim. I know what I am doing, just be patient," I replied as I pulled his hardened cock into my mouth.

Eddie allowed me to take my time and not push which meant more than I could ever express. For a guy on the brink to have to hold it while the girl figures it out has to suck. I dropped my head onto his hardened length and when I hit the back of his throat I wanted to gag, but he flicked my clit with his tongue and I focused in on what he was doing.

He always had a way of knowing what I needed when I needed it and I wanted and needing to accomplish this. To put Kurt behind me once and for all, and with Eddie I believed I could. He helped me heal and I didn't trust anyone the way I trusted him. He may have come into my life on a lie set up by my dad, but he stayed because he was exactly what I needed.

I continued by moving my hand up and down his rigid column as he pushed my hips down till I was sure I was suffocating him. I pulled him out of my mouth to run my tongue down his shaft and then quickly put him back in my mouth and swallowed down on him when he hit the back.

I tried to wiggle and squirm away from his mouth as my orgasm got closer. I wanted us to come together, and he wasn't ready. I worked him hard and faster trying to get us there. I pulled my hips up only for him to wrap his arms around my waist and hold me hostage to his tongue.

I screamed around his cock as I tried to hold back.

"Damn it woman! Just let go, come on my tongue," Eddie demanded and just like that I did.

As an orgasm more powerful than the sun shined down on me and exploded through my body I had nowhere to go as he held me there. I pulled his cock from my mouth as my nails dug into his thighs.

"Eddie," I shouted as the waves pounced into me one by one by one. I put his cock back into my mouth and quickly pulled him to the back of my throat. I felt him swell, at the same time a new orgasm formed in my horizon.

"Eddie," I called out, but he didn't stop his relentless onslaught. "I can't it's too -,"

I screamed again as he twirled his tongue. Holding me in place with one hand he pushed a finger inside my pussy who gripped onto it life a life raft, and then he pushed one finger into my ass. I cried out as he pushed me into places I had only been with him.

He swelled further in my mouth and the closer he got the faster his fingers moved in me. I thought my body was going to burst into flames or expire and leave me as a pile of ash.

Eddie grunted with the first spirt into my mouth. I swallowed it down and cupped his balls that had tightened up. I listened to his groan in ecstasy as I milked him for every last drop I could have, then without realizing it I came. It took me up to the land of euphoria to crash and explode out to every nerve ending.

If I could die by a single orgasm this would have been the one as my body thrummed, and I moaned, unable to make words or coherent thoughts. He had stolen my breath from me and his tongue continued it onslaught while I came down from my high slowly and when I found the ability to breathe again he picked me up and turned me around to lay with him.

"I'm truly sorry I wouldn't let you in," I whispered as my breathing settle and the stars lit up in the sky. Brooklyn's dinner would have to wait till the next night because I couldn't feel my legs. I listened to the heart beating beneath my ear knowing that this is where home was.

"I'm sorry I wasn't there when your parents passed, but I am so proud of you handling it on your own the way you did. Their service was beautiful and your eulogy truly was a celebration of their life."

"I just spoke from the heart. Something you taught me to do," I replied and Eddie placed a kiss on my head. "Where does that leave us?"

"I don't want to be your boyfriend because you can be loud, obnoxious, and a little flaky, and you run from commitment, Eddie stated with a hint of sarcasm, but then his voice took a serious tone. "But I love you, and am willing to work on it with you if you are."

I leaned up and placed a kiss on his lips. This was my happily ever after that I was comfortable with and my mom would have to wait on a son in law a little longer while we figured this thing out.

"I don't want to be your girlfriend because you are an asshat and that's contagious. I want to try monogamy and dating?"

"You pick where and I'll pick when," Eddie replied and the decision had been made. We were not together as a couple in the way most people would expect us to be, but what we have worked and I wasn't throwing it away.

"Eddie," I whispered as I started falling asleep under the tree.

"Do you think it's odd that I am no longer as angry and bitter as I was when you met me?"

"No Kate, I think you just needed someone capable of time and patience, but when he didn't come you wound up with me," Eddie stated with a light laugh and I smacked his arm. "Kate we don't have to have a happily ever after like books and movies show. I love what we have because it is what works for us. We will argue and fight. We will throw things at each other, but at the end of the day when you are curled up on me like this. That is the moment that I know we will always be together even if we don't have it planned out."

"I like the non-plan plan," I softly spoke as I twirled my fingers up and down his arm. "You fall, I fall, right?" I asked.

"Every single day, but Kate," Eddie gruffly started. "I won't ever let you fall."

"Hey Eddie," I said as I stretched my legs and laid one over his.

"Yea?"

"I'm addicted to you," I admitted.

"Good," he replied with a kiss on my head. "It will make keeping you for fifty more years easy if you need a daily fix from me," he laughed, and turned pushing me onto my back. I spread my legs welcoming him in as he climbed on top.

"You sure you are ready to ride my rollercoaster of crazy?" I asked and Eddie pushed into me.

"Always," Eddie replied and I dug my nails into his shoulders as I was still really sensitive from having just orgasmed.

"If you think you are ready then grab your keys, get in, buckle up, and hold on because I am a hell of a ride," I whispered as I pushed to roll him over.

"Let's see what you got Miss Huntington, or shall I spank you for trying to be the boss again?"

There no need for foreplay now, just a need to have him. He knew it because he could read right through me and let me do things my way, but eventually he would take control and give me what I longed for. Him. I gasped for breath when I realized he had pushed his way into a forever spot in my heart.

"I love you, Eddie," I moaned into the night air as my pussy stroked his cock up and down.

"I love you, Kate," he replied, and pulled me down to place my nipples in his mouth. I swore I would never get enough of him as long as I lived.

Note from the Author

Hope you have enjoyed Chase Me, and seeing how Eddie and Kate's relationship came together. I know it is not like my other books, but that is because no two character stories are the same. You can follow their progress in my other series:

Brooklyn Series

Water Series

If you loved this story you should follow me, and see what I write next.

FB Page: http://goo.gl/JUe0lZ

Street Team: https://goo.gl/5g9gcG

Fan Group: https://goo.gl/CMB9cb

Twitter: @AuthorEYork

Amazon Page: http://goo.gl/4grbpK